MW00941615

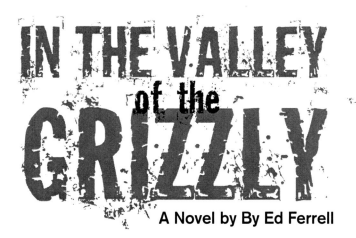

# IN THE VALLEY of the GRIZZLY

## A Novel by By Ed Ferrell

Alaska Northwest Books®

Library of Congress Cataloging-in-Publication Data available upon request.

Cover design by Elizabeth Watson

Interior design by Boven Design

Edited by Michelle McCann

**Alaska Northwest Books®**

An imprint of Graphic Arts Books

P.O. Box 56118

Portland, OR 97238-6118

# DEDICATION

Ed Ferrell came to Alaska as a young man in search of the last frontier. The wilderness, adventure, and stark truth of this great untamed place captured his imagination. He had tremendous admiration and respect for the early Alaskan pioneers and native peoples who embraced such a harsh land. He also loved a good story, especially if it involved survival against all odds.

*In the Valley of the Grizzly* is his expression of those loves and is dedicated to all who yearn for the frontier.

—William & Patricia Ferrell

# ACKNOWLEDGMENTS

Cyrus Peck, Jr., a Tlingit Medicine Man, provided authentic information on clans, and the spiritual nature of Tlingit traditions. Dave Williams was reared in a traditional Tlingit home and shared his knowledge with me. For early-day flying stories in the North Country, I relied on Stewart Adams who flew for Alaska Coastal and Alaska Airlines. For information on the de Havilland Beaver, I am indebted to Phil McRee, former Air Force instructor, and to Bob Jacobsen, president of Wings of Alaska. I wish to thank Dr. Joseph Lenox, Dr. Robert Michaud, and Dr. Henry Akiyama for information on head and scalp wounds. Duane Petersen, biologist and Alaska big game guide, and John Joyce, biologist with Alaska Department of Fish and Game, provided me information on bear behavior.

My brothers, George and Wayne Little, for bow hunting techniques and to Micah Nutt, for information on snowshoes. My thanks go also to my daughter, Patricia Ferrell, for reading the manuscript and making suggestions from the perspective of a children's librarian. I also express my gratitude to my wife, Nancy Warren Ferrell, for the hours she spent proofreading and editing. In addition to being a national book reviewer, she has published numerous books and articles. Consequently, Nancy brought to the writing process a professional background.

I wish to acknowledge the following authors, past and present, for their works on Alaska: John Holzworth, author of *The Wild Grizzlies of Alaska* (permission to use the Hasselborg story was granted by Dr. Jean Holzworth, DVM and Elizabeth Holzworth Gilliam); Nora Marks Dauenhauer and Richard Dauenhauer authors of *Haa Kusteeyi Our Culture, Tlingit Life Stories*; George Thornton Emmons author of *The Tlingit Indians*; Aurel Krause *The Tlingit Indians*; and Dr. Cyrus E. Peck author of *The Tides People*.

—Ed Ferrell

# CHAPTER 1

**The Beaver's engine** fired in a steady rhythm. From the cockpit, Ben watched the British Columbia wilderness pass under him. Excited, he turned to his grandfather in the back seat. Shouting over the roar of the motor, Ben said, "Hey, Grandpa, great country. Haven't seen a road since we left Wrangell. Gonna be some great fishing."

"Land of our ancestors, Bennie," the old man said proudly. "Our people came into this place thousands of years ago." His voice carried the soft accent of the Tlingit people. Ben groaned to himself, thinking, *Grandpa, I'm here to fish not to hear about our ancestors. I know you mean well, but . . .*

Ben checked his watch. They were three hours out of Wrangell. He grinned to himself, recalling how the trip originated. It came out of the blue.

He and Grandfather happened to be in Dan's office, a shack on the edge of the airstrip, to arrange a fly-in fishing trip. Dan was on the short-wave radio talking to the owner of the Tahltan Creek Mine.

"Thought I'd fly up and give you boys a few lessons in the finer points of draw poker."

"Come on up, Fly Boy," the Canadian accent responded. "Us poor Canucks would be grateful for any instructions on that noble game. Bring plenty of money, eh! Yank."

Dan signed off and issued the invitation: "You guys want to take a short hop to Tahltan Creek and thereabouts?" Ben smiled. *A short hop? Only in Alaska would a pilot fly 200 miles just to play poker.* Crossing his fingers, excited by the invitation, Ben looked at Grandfather.

Grinning at Ben's obvious eagerness to go, the old man nodded yes.

"Okay," said Dan, "I'll be fueled and ready to go tomorrow morning about seven. You won't need sleeping bags or food. We'll stay in the bunkhouse and Mrs. Dalton will take care of the cooking."

Ben smiled to himself, recalling the good-natured banter between Dan and the Canadian. *Well, you guys can play poker. Me?* Ben cocked his head thinking. *No, Grandpa would never let me play. The first thing I'm going to do when we land is to grab my fishing rod.* Ben turned to the pilot, "I bet those rivers and lakes have never been fished."

Dan grinned, "Anxious to try out that new rod and reel your Grandfather got you? When we finish this little side jaunt, we'll head for the mine. I think I've found some good sheep country for my hunters. We'll be in Tahltan Creek tonight and then three days of nothing but great fishing and good eating. The grayling are just begging to be caught."

"I'm ready to wet a hook. Man! That's big lonesome country out there!"

Looking over at Ben, Dan said, "Yeah it's big, wild, and beautiful, Ben.

Just the way the Man Upstairs made it. The last of its kind."

"You could put a dozen Washingtons down there, and they wouldn't make a dent," Ben replied, excited to see the unbroken wilderness.

Dan laughed a good-natured laugh. "I'm not sure about a dozen. Washington is a pretty big state. But there's a lot of country in here and not a lot of people. This part of British Columbia hasn't even been completely surveyed."

"No kidding?"

"Gospel truth." Dan grinned at Ben's enthusiasm.

Scared by the roar of the motor, a band of sheep scampered up a talus slope led by a big ram. Turning, the animal watched the plane.

Dan sized up the animal. "Full curl. He's a trophy. I got a client that will pay some big bucks for him."

"See the sheep, Grandpa?"

"Big Horn, Bennie. Should be mountain goats in here too. Look on the cliffs. Goats are generally higher on the mountain than sheep."

Ben searched the cliffs for goats, but something about Dan nagged at him. He studied the pilot. Dan didn't seem concerned about anything. He sat in a half-slouch, one hand on the yoke, looking over the country, a pipe clamped in his jaws, a derelict Stetson perched on the back of his head.

*What is it about Dan?* Ben wondered, but he couldn't quite put his finger on it.

Giving up on trying to place Dan, Ben relaxed and watched the land.

Below an unnamed river poured through a gorge. "Dan, do you see those deer swimming the river? Must be a couple hundred." Fascinated, Ben pointed them out.

"Yeah, I spotted them. Caribou, Ben. Small herd, probably trying to get away from the flies. Come the fall migrations, you'll see them by the tens of thousands."

"Man, doesn't look like a small herd to me. That's pretty swift water. Caribou must be good swimmers."

"They are Ben. Their hair is hollow. Helps to keep them afloat. But a lot drown in these rivers."

Turning, Ben looked at his grandfather. "Did you see the caribou Grandpa?"

"Sure did, Bennie. They're the buffalo of the north country."

"Grandpa, I can't believe all the bear, moose, sheep, and caribou I've seen. "You've got sharp eyes," Grandfather smiled, pleased Ben was enjoying himself.

"It must be my Indian blood, Grandpa," Ben joked.

Grandfather's smile disappeared. "Don't make light of our people, Bennie."

"*Sorry.*" *Forgot how touchy you are, Grandpa. I love you, but you take all that Indian pride stuff way too seriously. Just a lot of old stories and super-stitions. The old ways are history. Maybe your way Grandpa, but not my way.*

Shrugging off his feelings, Ben's eyes were again drawn to the wild country stretching before him.

"Hey Ben, look at the grizzly."

Ben leaned forward trying to see where the pilot was pointing.

"I can't see him, Dan."

"Hold on, I'll swing around on your side." Dan banked the plane and made another pass along the mountain. "There, at the edge of the water."

"I see him! I see him!"

The grizzly stood near a glacier pool, a magnificent blue-grey animal, his silky fur silvering in the wind. The lord of the wilderness.

Awed, Grandfather said, "He is the Spirit Grandfather of all bears."

"I think he knows he's top dog, or in his case, top bear." Dan laughed at his own joke.

"Dan, it is best we do not laugh at *Hootz*. It shows disrespect."

"Sorry Cyrus. No disrespect meant."

Ben knew his grandfather held the grizzly in great reverence. He remembered as a small boy snuggling up to him, listening to him tell stories in his Tlingit accent about the bear people. An ancient legend told of their kinship. A Tlingit woman married a bear and bore many children. From that time on, whenever a Tlingit met a bear it was addressed as brother. The person would say, "Brother, I do not want to disturb you, and I mean you no harm. Let us go in peace."

Looking down at the grizzly, Ben thought, *That's a good kid's story Grandpa, but he doesn't look like my brother.*

Suddenly, sputtering and backfiring, the engine quit. Startled, Ben shot a look at Dan. He was doing something at the controls. Thundering back into life, the motor throbbed with a steady beat. Pulse pounding in his ears, Ben eased back into his seat.

Now sitting erect, Dan gripped the yoke with both hands. "Guys, I'm gonna get us some altitude." Pushing in the throttle and pulling back on the yoke, the pilot climbed out of the valley. Several times, Dan leaned over looking out of Ben's side window.

Apprehensive, Ben asked, "What are you looking for, Dan?"

"For a place to put this bird down, Ben. She's not running right. Got to check her out." Ben's throat tightened. Not sure of how serious the situation was, he searched for a lake or clearing.

With a series of noisy explosions, the motor quit again. The prop jerked to a stop and this time the plane started to fall. Switching tanks, Dan tried the starter. Ben could hear it clunk. The Pratt and Whitney fired into life once more.

Body tense, Ben leaned forward, listening to the motor with every fiber of his body. It stopped again and an eerie silence filled the cockpit. When Dan tried the starter again the motor belched black smoke, the propeller windmilled.

"Mayday! Mayday! Mayday!" Dan yelled into the mike. "This is Taggart, Niner, Niner, Charlie! Red and yellow de Havilland Beaver, Devil's Elbow bears 15 degrees, magnetic distance 150 miles. Engine trouble. Mayday!

Mayday! Mayday!"

Dropping the mike, Dan tried the starter again. Clunk! Clunk! Clunk! "Start, damn it, start!"

With his eyes glued to the window, Ben searched for a landing spot. Dense timber carpeted the valley floor. A rock ridge ran along one side of the valley. Dan nosed the Beaver down to pick up air speed and to get control of the falling plane, the wind making a whistling sound on the aluminum body.

Looking out the windshield, Ben spotted a lake at the head of the valley, nestled at the edge of a ridge, faced with cliffs, topped with trees.

"A lake! A lake!" Ben shouted, pointing. "Look, Dan, that ridge to your left. See it?"

"Yeah," Dan nodded.

Ben thought: *It's miles away. We'll never make it. Oh please God help us . . . help us!*

Chest heaving, Ben leaned forward, his eyes locked on the distant lake, willing the plane to the water. The Beaver hurtled toward the ridge. Sheer granite walls looking like a medieval castle rushed toward them.

Gripping the seat, heart pounding, Ben watched the cliffs. Dark masses of green abruptly took shapes, forming trees. Tight throated, Ben couldn't breath. Palisades leaped in front of the plane. Fear-numbing adrenalin shot through him. Granite cliffs filled the windshield.

"We're going in!"

# CHAPTER 2

**The Beaver scraped the trees** as it cleared the cliffs. A screeching and pounding of aluminum filled the cabin. The bush plane shuddered from the hits. Dan pulled up the nose to cut the air speed. Flaring the plane out, he dropped it onto the surface. The Beaver hit with a metallic slap, the impact shooting geysers of water and plant debris into the air. Pitching and rocking, the aircraft bounced to a stop, water pouring off the windows.

Dan's hands gripped the yoke. The sound of dripping water broke the silence. "Anyone hurt?" He looked over at Ben.

Ben shook his head no. He couldn't talk.

"Cyrus?"

"I'm fine Daniel. Shook up a little."

Hard-faced, Dan stepped out on a pontoon. Unfastening the oar from a bracket, he worked the plane into shore. "The gas had water and rust in it. I told that kid to strain the fuel. Damn near got us killed."

Ben unhooked his seat belt and eased out on the pontoon, grabbed a strut and swung down to the beach. The plane smelled of gasoline, mangled water plants, and lake mud. Torn plants floated on the lake surface. He couldn't believe they'd made it down in one piece. Relief poured over him like a warm shower.

Ben savored the feeling of land under his feet. He eyed the lake and the area around it, confirming it was real and he was still alive. It felt good just to breath.

Then the fear hit him again.

Ben's knees buckled. Stumbling, he leaned against the wing to steady himself. Grandfather got out behind Ben, and took him by the arm. "How you holding up, Bennie?"

"Lousy!"

Ben walked over to a tree and took a leak. On the beach, Dan and Grandfather stood near the plane relieving themselves. *I see I'm not the only one that got the pee scared out of him.*

Buttoning up his Levis, Ben looked down the valley. On his left, the lake spilled out over boulders forming a shallow river that ran along the cliff side of the valley. The dark cliffs paralleled the river as far as he could see. On the other side, the country flattened out, giving way to meadows, ponds, and then to timbered ridges and hills. Willows grew along the flats next to the river. A warm breeze lifted off the land carrying with it the earthy, spicy smell of the wilderness.

*Nearly became a permanent part of this place.* Ben took a few more minutes to try to get his mind set to normal again. Then he strode back to the plane. Grandfather sat on a rock, sharpening his hunting knife.

"You still O.K. Grandpa?"

Looking up at Ben, the old man nodded. "I'm fine, Bennie," he said, feeling the edge of the knife with his thumb. "Dan's a good pilot. Flew one of those fighter planes during the war. At my age not too many things bother me. Besides, the owl didn't call my name."

Ben hadn't heard the expression for years and searched his memory. Some of the old people still believed the owl was the death messenger. He would call your name when your time came.

"He didn't call my name either," Ben teased. "But I think I heard him hoot a couple of times."

"Grandson, do not make fun of the old ways."

Ben chided him. "Grandpa it's 1950, not 1850. Time to join the 20th Century."

"I lived by the old ways for eighty years, Bennie, and it hasn't hurt me." Ben thought: *It hurt us Grandpa. Your old ways nearly cost you a daughter and a grandson.*

Dan had the mike in hand, trying to contact the dispatcher. "This is Taggart, Niner, Niner, Charlie. Do you copy Wrangell? Over. Taggart, Niner, Niner, Charlie. Do you copy? Over."

After a few tries, Dan gave up and joined Grandfather and Ben. "Couldn't raise anyone in Wrangell or at the Tahltan Creek Mine. Bad country for radio. Too many mountains. Doubt if the Mayday got through." Dan eased down on a boulder, filled his pipe and lit up. Sighing, he exhaled a puff of fragrant smoke. "Nothing like a good pipe to settle a man's nerves."

*The smell! The pipe smell! That's it! That's what I couldn't put together about Dan. Dad smoked the same kind of tobacco.* The fragrant smoke triggered a painful flashback for Ben.

Nineteen forty-two, World War II. Ben was seven years old standing with his mom and dad outside the Seattle train station. Dad was being shipped overseas. With his pipe in one hand, Dad hugged him. The smell of pipe smoke wrapped around Ben like a blanket. Burying his head in his dad's shoulder, Ben wouldn't let him go. Mom pulled him away crying. The train whistle blew. "I've gotta go, honey. I'll write." Dad kissed her again, shouldered his duffle, and joined the other paratroopers boarding the train. Turning around, Dad waved.

Ben never saw him again.

Dan interrupted Ben's thoughts, "That landing still spooking you, Ben?" The smell of the pipe nearly brought tears to Ben's eyes. He had to turn away so Dan couldn't see his face.

"No, I'm O.K."

# CHAPTER 3

**Dan pointed at the plane,** "Let's get this bird airborne again. I'll have to drain the lines and refuel. You guys can unload the gas cans. They're in the cargo hatch."

Knocking out his pipe ashes, he continued, "While you're doing that, I'll check the plane for damage, probably O.K. It's built like a tank. Scraped the trees pretty hard when we came over the ridge."

Dan hunkered down on the pontoons and inspected the undercarriage. He ran his hand along each strut looking for fractures and breaks and checked the bolts connecting the pontoons to the body. Then he crawled from under the plane grinning. "Got a dent in the starboard pontoon, but this baby will fly again. It'll take awhile to drain the tanks and fuel lines and get the water out. "

Dan looked over at Ben. "This would be a good time to try out your new fishing outfit, Ben. Looks like a good fishing spot. Doubt it's ever been fished. It'll get your mind off things." Grandfather nodded his head in agreement.

Eager to try his new rod, Ben assembled and tested it. "Great action!"

Grandfather smiled, pleased that Ben liked it. Unscrewing a jar of salted herring bellies, he sliced off a thin strip.

"Here," he said, giving it to Ben. Grandfather read the water and selected a spot where the current eddied around a boulder. "Now I'll show you how Indians fish." Casting out near a large boulder at the outlet, Grandfather started retrieving the lure. Speaking softly and respectfully, he prayed in Tlingit for success. Ben recognized the fish prayer from his childhood. His Tlingit was rusty, but he got most of it. Grandfather said: "Forgive me for wanting to harm you. But I am hungry, and I need your flesh. I will not waste anything."

Ben shook his head. *Grandpa, I don't think the fish care if you are hungry. For damn sure they don't want to be gutted, fried, and chewed up.*

Embarrassed by the prayer, Ben followed a game trail through clumps of willows to a point of land that jutted into the lake to form a cove. Yellow water lilies edged the cove; their heart-shaped leaves glistened in the sun. Clumps of willows grew along the shore.

Ben flipped the lure into the current that flowed around the point. Instantly, the rod arched and a fish erupted out of the water, trailing silver bubbles. "Got one!" Ben shouted, setting the hook. The grayling fought all the way in until the silver-grey fish lay flopping on the beach, pink gills pumping. "Hey, Grandpa! How's that for the first cast on my new rod. Wow! Man, this is the way to fish. That lure barely hit the surface."

Grandfather looked up smiling and nodded his head.

Ben examined the fish. With his finger, he lifted the purple, sail-like dorsal fin. The iridescent sides sparkled in the sun. "A beauty. Looks kinda like a trout." Hefting it, Ben estimated the fish weighed about a pound. "Not bad for a city boy." For a few hectic minutes, Ben took a grayling with every cast. He couldn't believe it. Then, abruptly, the fish stopped biting.

After several more casts, he picked up his string of fish. Admiring his catch, Ben started back. As he walked along the edge of the lake, Ben could see schools of grayling in the clear water, darting along the shallows. He could hear a soft breeze whistling through the willows.

The roar of the Beaver's engine shattered the stillness. Relieved to hear the big 450-horse Pratt and Whitney engine firing again, Ben walked over to the plane. Dan's tools lay strewn across the ground. He was adjusted something. The motor settled into a throbbing rhythm. Cutting the switch, Dan wiped his hands on a rag. "I see you broke that new rod in, Ben."

"Sure did! Best fishing I ever had." Ben grinned, still excited by his success, the near fatal landing all but forgotten. "I can hardly wait until they start biting again."

Dan looked around. "It's getting late and this is a good place to camp tonight. We'll hit the mine tomorrow after I've had a chance to test the fly-fishing here. We'll need the grub box. It's got chow and cooking gear in it." Dan opened the cargo hatch, pulled out a wooden box and handed it to Ben. Then he took out an army packsack and set it on the beach.

"Ben, some old-timers don't like people using their axe," he said, grinning at Grandfather. The old man nodded in agreement. "So, use this." Dan held a saw up, a tool with a curved metal frame, a blade stretched between the ends.

Dan climbed into the cockpit and clicked the lap belt. "O.K. I'm ready to roll. Give me a shove, guys. I've got to get this bird in the air and cancel that Mayday before every bush pilot in the Yukon is out looking for us."

Dan turned the starter switch. The engine thundered into life. Ben and Grandfather grabbed the wing struts and pushed the plane off the beach. Revving up the motor, Dan adjusted the RPMs. Skimming down the lake, the Beaver got up on the step and lifted off. Dan waggled the wings and gave them a thumb's up as he flew by. Ben watched the red and yellow plane until it disappeared over the mountain.

# CHAPTER 4

Lonely and apprehensive about Dan's leaving, Ben walked along the lakeshore, unable to shake his dark feelings. *Just my imagination. Dan's been flying this country since the war. He'll be back.*

Suddenly, Ben stopped. Embedded in the sand, large tracks with claw marks led along the lake. Bear! Anxiously, Ben scanned the lake and the edge of the timber. Glancing up, he saw his grandfather approaching.

"Saw you looking at the tracks. Just ran across them myself." He crouched down to study the ground. "A grizzly. Male. A big one for this country. Weighs maybe 700 to 900 pounds. About eight feet tall, maybe taller. I think he came up from the coast. Bears are a lot bigger there. They feed on salmon."

"Hold on, Grandpa. How do you know it's a male? Why couldn't it be a female?"

"It's a male. See the hind tracks? He peed in front of them." Grandfather pointed with a stick at the damp spot. "A sow pees in back of her hind legs. Not quite dry. I'd say he came through here about an hour ago Probably scared off by the plane."

"Got it." Ben frowned. "But the size? How can you tell that by the track?"

*Come on, Grandpa that's just Indian talk.* "Look at my footprint. Can you tell how much I weigh and how tall I am?"

Grandfather stared at Ben, hurt by his attitude. In a sad voice he said, "I spent most of my eighty years in the bush. I've seen hundreds of bears both dead and alive, so I've got some experience in estimating the size and weight of bears. These tracks are about eight inches wide. You figure a foot in height for every inch. Makes him around eight foot tall. See how deep the tracks are? Shows he's a big, heavy animal."

"What I see in your tracks, Bennie, is a smart-alecky kid, who, if he pays attention and lives to grow up, will be a *skookum* man like his dad."

"O.K. Grandpa," Ben replied, feeling a little ashamed of his remark. He thought of his dad. True, he was a big, strong man.

Grandfather continued, "Look here, part of the right front foot is missing." Puzzling over the deformed paw, the old man thought for a minute. "Bear's been in a trap. Looks like he might've torn off his toes pulling them out of the trap. He may have good reason to hate people. Bears are very smart and have good memories."

Keep your eyes open, Bennie. Don't wander off too far."

"Fat chance," Ben said, looking around.

Grandfather shook his head. "That landing shook up my old brain. Forgot to take out my rifle. Might need that old Winchester. But I did get my axe. Let's head back and see what's in the grub box that'll go with fish."

Grandfather checked through the box. "We've got bacon, potatoes, eggs, and tea. We won't go hungry. Now, I'll give you a lesson on fire making."

"Grandpa," Ben protested, "I know how to build a fire. I learned that in the Scouts."

"No, you know how to build a Boy Scout fire. So you and your sweetheart can stand around and roast marshmallows or cook hot dogs."

" I don't have a sweetheart."

"Well, you will."

Sighing, Ben thought of Jeannie, the brown-haired girl who sat in front of him in his math class last year. She was smart, cute, and always smelled like she just got out of the shower. Ben thought maybe she liked him, but he had never worked up the courage to ask her for a date.

Walking over to a birch tree, Grandfather stripped off a sheet of fuzzy bark. "Use this for tinder. Burns plenty hot. Look at this birch," he said, fingering a fungus growth. He chopped it off and showed it to Ben. "This wood is good for making fires when it's dry, it catches a spark easily." He then used a stick to collect sap and smeared it on the cut mark.

"Why are you doing that, Grandpa?" Ben asked, puzzled.

"Sap protects the tree from diseases. Gives it a chance to heal. If you injure the earth, you should try to heal it. It's the way of the *Kolosh*."

"*Kolosh*, Grandpa?" *Shouldn't have asked him. I'll probably get a lecture about the old ways. It's just a tree, Grandpa. There's a forest full of them, Jeez.*

"It is the ancient name of our people, the true name." Grandfather said with pride.

*I knew it!*

From a stand of dead, lodgepole pine, Grandfather selected a tree streaked with yellow sap. "Make your kindling out of this," he said, pointing to the resin streaks. "Good fire starter."

With the easy strokes of a skilled axe man, Grandfather felled the tree and cut it into sections, littering the ground with V-shaped chunks. Then he selected a yellowed, crusted piece and split it into kindling. "When you use my axe, don't nick it," he cautioned.

"Grandpa," Ben protested, "I won't nick your axe. I know how to use tools." Grumbling, Ben thought, *Still treats me like a little kid. Why is he showing me all this stuff? I came up here to fish, not to play Daniel Boone.*

Grandfather supervised as Ben built a fire next to a boulder. "Here, take my knife and cut the bark into thin pieces. Use a piece of the firewood to cut it on."

Ben rolled his eyes, "I know, Grandpa. I won't nick your axe."
Ignoring Ben's comment, Grandfather continued. "You'll need a handful of tinder." When he was satisfied that Ben had enough tinder cut, he said, "O.K., fluff it up and arrange the kindling teepee style over the tinder." Ben grumbled to himself, but built a teepee. "You got it. Light it up!" He handed Ben a book of matches.

Grandfather made Ben nervous. The first match sputtered out. The next one flared up and he touched it to the tinder. The fluffy birch wad caught and flamed up, igniting the kindling. Blue-orange flames licked at the yellow streaked-wood and exploded into a roaring fire. Ben piled wood on the fire. The dry lodgepole pine snapped and popped, shooting sparks into the air.

"We're going to be out of matches pretty quick," Grandfather said, tucking the matchbook into his coat pocket. "I found these in the grub box. Had matches in my gear, but left them on the plane. Can't believe I did that. We'll have to go with flint and steel. Use the knife for a sparker. I haven't seen any flint around here, but we'll find something that'll spark."

"Bennie," Grandfather said looking at him. "I know you can generally make a fire. But to stay alive in this country. . ." he waved his arm at the horizon to show the vastness of the land, ". . . you've got to be able to make a fire at anytime, at any place. Fall through the ice at 40-below, you're dead in an hour without one. You've got to get a fire going in five minutes or your fingers get so cold you can't strike a match. Not too many second chances in the bush. Always have tinder and kindling with you. Never leave camp without your knife, axe, and tinder."

When the fire burned down, Grandfather raked the coals together for a cooking fire. "While I'm cooking supper, cut some more firewood. And don't nick my axe."

Ben cringed.

The savory odors of sizzling bacon, fried grayling, and steaming tea made Ben ravenously hungry. After two plates, he couldn't eat anymore.

"Great food, Grandpa."

"Camp fire food always tastes better. Eat up, Bennie. I saved some for Dan."

"No, I can't eat anymore." Contented, Ben leaned against a rock next to the fire, drinking a cup of tea—strong, black, hot, and sweet. But he couldn't shake the feeling that something was wrong.

*What's taking Dan so long?*

# CHAPTER 5

**Worried about Dan, Ben checked** his watch. It was ten o'clock. "Grandpa, shouldn't Dan be back by now? He's been gone a long time."

"Dan could come in anytime, Bennie. Lot of daylight up here in the summer. It'll get a little dusky around midnight."

Ben shook his head. "Things just don't feel right, Grandpa. Dan's been gone four hours."

Grandfather searched the sky for a minute. Then he turned and looked at Ben. "Yes, Dan has been gone too long, Bennie. I didn't want to bring it up, but you have a right to know. He's probably down someplace. Nothing we can do about it. We can only hope he'll make it back."

"But don't count him out," Grandfather cautioned. "Bush pilots carry emergency supplies: rifles, snowshoes, fishing rods, sleeping bags, camping gear. If Dan walks away from the landing, he has a chance. It's hard country, Bennie, but Dan's a hard man. If anybody can make it, he can." Ben felt only slightly comforted by his grandfather's confident words.

"Right now we need to take care of us. First thing, we need to do is set up camp."

Grandfather pointed at a place near the fire. "Dan has our sleeping bags, so we'll have to make do. We'll put our beds next to this big rock. It'll get chilly later on, but if we keep a fire going all night the rock will reflect the heat."

Grandfather picked up his axe and motioned for Ben to follow. Striding ahead, he stopped by a stand of spruce. "White spruce—very springy, makes a good mattress." He selected trees, cutting a few boughs from each.

Ben packed them to the camp, cleaned the bed site of rocks, and arranged the boughs on the ground. "Good enough, Ben. If we cover ourselves with more spruce, we'll stay warm."

"Grizzlies are out at night. We'll have to get up to throw wood on the fire." Glancing around at the camp, he continued, "I must be getting old. It's still early, but I'm going to bed."

Grandfather lay down on the spruce mattress and covered himself with boughs. "Just like my bed at home." From out of the twilight came the cry of a wolf pack, a lonely haunting sound. Sitting up, Grandfather looked down the valley. A second chorus of howls rose, ending in a long moaning cry.

"They're on a moose kill, Bennie."

"You can tell by their howl?"

"Yes, that's what the wolves are saying."

Ben listened, trying to make something out of the howls. "They sound spooky to me."

"Got some pups with them. Hear the yelps and whines?"

"Yeah. Do they mean anything?"

"No. They're just learning the calls."

"The pups sound like pups, but the rest sound kinda dangerous."

"Wolves generally stay clear of people. Besides, *Gooch* will not harm you," Grandfather assured Ben. "They are your clan."

Ben hadn't heard the Tlingit word for wolf in years. His mother belonged to the Wolf clan and, under Tlingit law, so did he. Ben had never given the clans much thought. That was something the old people kept track of, something to do with who you marry.

"This bunch will probably have one good feed on the moose and then leave it."

"Why do wolves do that Grandpa? It doesn't seem right, leaving all that meat to rot."

"When they leave the kill, other animals feed on it. Nothing goes to waste. Even the bones are eaten by mice. In the old days, the wolf would be your . . ." Grandfather stopped, searching for an English equivalent for the words, " . . . totem spirit animal. Your house is *Gooch Kanlye*, wolf den."

*You just don't give up, do you Grandpa? If the kids at school ever found out my clan name, they'd call me something dumb like Wolf Boy or Wolfie. Already get called Chief, Tonto, Kimo Sabe, and Geronimo. Had problems with the Indian thing.*

Ben's frustration boiled over. "Grandpa, why did you hate my dad?" Startled, Grandfather sat back up. "I didn't hate your dad. Travis was a fine man."

"But you didn't want Mom to marry him, did you?" Ben asked, anger in his voice. "My dad was a good guy."

"Bennie, I wanted Nora to marry within the tribe. But I was wrong. So wrong. And I said some mean things to her."

Yeah, Ben thought, *Mom told me about that. You didn't want her to marry Dad because he was white. She got mad, stormed upstairs, packed a suitcase, stomped back downstairs and out the door, slamming it behind her.*

"Later I found out they got married in Seattle. You were two years old before I even knew I had a grandson." Grandfather closed his eyes so long Ben thought he had dozed off.

"I'm sorry, Bennie." It came out so quiet that Ben could barely hear it over the popping fire. "Travis was a fine man. After he died, I asked your Mom to come back home to be with her family. Those were some of the happiest days of my life."

Ben could see Grandfather was hurt. Relenting, he said, "It's history now, Grandpa. Let's get some sleep." Lying on his back, Ben stared into the sky, listening for the roar of the Pratt and Whitney. *Dan should have been back hours ago. But it's still light. He could come in any time. We can't be stuck out here forever.*

# CHAPTER 6

**Ben awoke to the early** morning calm. Careful not to disturb Grandfather, he got out of bed and walked to the edge of the lake, searching the sky. *Please, God, I want to hear the roar of that Pratt and Whitney motor again.* Instead, a loon's eerie yodel rose from the lake.

Grandfather walked up. "*Awasa*, grandson," he said greeting Ben in Tlingit and handing him a cup of tea.

"I don't want anything, Grandpa. I'm too worried about Dan."

"I know Bennie. I'm worried too. I made the tea extra strong. It'll make you feel better. Here, take it." Grandfather looked pale and drawn, his movements unsteady. Getting up, Ben took him by the arm. "Are you all right?"

"I'm fine. It just takes me awhile to get going in the morning. Once I'm up, I'm fine. Now let me go. I'll put some grub on."

"Grandpa, this is 1950. Planes don't just disappear without a big search. Someone is going to come looking for us!"

"I doubt it, Bennie. Not in this part of the country. Dan told the mine people he was coming up to play poker. I don't think he contacted them about a change in plans.

"He tried, but he couldn't raise anyone at the mine or at Telegraph Creek."

"Well then, no one's gonna know where we are. After we passed Telegraph Creek, Dan decided to swing through here. Wanted to find some virgin country for his hunters. The mine is in the Cassiar Mountains, a couple hundred miles northwest of here. If Wrangell never answered, then it's doubtful the Mayday ever got through. We know the folks in Telegraph Creek saw us because Dan waggled his wings and waved as we flew over. So, any searches will be between Telegraph Creek and Tahltan Creek."

Numbed, Ben couldn't speak. *This only happens in books. Not in real life. We may not get out of here.*

Grandfather continued. "This is an unforgiving country, Bennie. But our people lived here for 10,000 years and they survived. So can we."

"I've been studying this out in my mind." With a stick, Grandfather drew a rough map in the sand, marking north with an arrow. "This valley runs roughly north," he said, pointing down the valley. "The Alcan Highway is north of us, but I'm not sure how far it is. The Stikine River is west of us and it runs south to the sea." He scratched a snaky, north-south line for the river and an "X" for Telegraph Creek, the nearest settlement.

"Dan said the Beaver makes . . .." Grandfather stopped, searching for the right word.

"Cruises, Grandpa. I think Dan said the Beaver cruises at 110 miles an hour, depending on the load and wind conditions."

"Well then, we were in the air two hours after we passed Telegraph Creek and turned east. That puts us a good 200 airplane miles east of Telegraph Creek. That'll be more like 300 hard walking miles to Telegraph Creek. This is plenty wild country."

"Three hundred miles!" *We're not walking out of this country, Grandpa. This can't be real.*

"Why can't we just head south for Wrangell and forget about Telegraph Creek. Wouldn't that be closer?"

"It might be closer, but the coast mountains and the ice fields are impassable. That's the reason the Indian people have always used the Stikine, Taku, or Yukon Rivers to get into the interior country."

Ben didn't know what to say. "Any people around here? There's gotta be somebody."

"I doubt it. Nothing to bring folks in here. Might be a few Tahltan families still living the old ways. Most of the tribe moved into the settlements during the war. No money in furs anymore.

We'll have to wait until freeze-up and walk out."

Ben challenged Grandfather. "Why can't we walk out now? Three hundred miles is the same frozen or unfrozen."

Grandfather sighed. "That's true, Bennie, but how are we going to get across those rivers we saw flying in? Remember the caribou?"

Ben pictured in his mind the caribou swimming the river through whirlpools and raging white water.

"Oh yeah," Ben said reluctantly. "I wouldn't want to try swimming them. Some of those rivers were pretty spooky. They scared me just flying over them." Ben looked away, trying to sort out his feelings.

"Let's worry about now, starting with the grub box." Grandfather opened the lid and inventoried the contents. "Not much here: tea, sugar, pepper, salt, half a slab of bacon and . . ." he paused, counting, ". . . six eggs, four potatoes, a couple cans of tobacco, pipe, towel, bar of soap, shaving mirror, razor, first aid kit, sewing kit, butcher knife, cups, plates, eating utensils, coffee pot, frying pan, my hunting knife, sharpening stone and file. That's it." He held up a wooden-handled table knife. "This is an old timer. We could make arrowheads out of these. You got anything, Bennie?"

"Just my fishing rod and Scout knife." Ben handed the knife to Grandfather. "It's not very sharp."

Grandfather checked the blade. "That's O.K., we can still use it. The awl will come in handy for punching holes in leather. Go see what's in Dan's pack."

The pack leaned against a tree where Dan had left it. As Ben opened the pack, he noticed writing on the side: Lt. Dan Taggart, AAF, 304th

"Grandpa, what does AAF stand for?"

"Army Air Force. I think the number was his unit."

Sadness came over Ben as he pulled out rubber waders. He knew what they were—his dad had a pair just like them. "This is Dan's fishing stuff. Here's the rod his dad gave him. I don't want to look through his stuff, Grandpa. I just don't feel right about it."

"Leave it for now. Let's look the country over to see what's out there to eat. But first, I will prepare myself. I must show respect to the animals so they will give their bodies to us."

Ben thought, *If all this Indian stuff makes you happy, I guess it's O.K. But the animals are going to need a little more persuasion . . . like a 30-06 rifle slug. I sure wish you hadn't left your Winchester on the plane.*

# CHAPTER 7

As Grandfather began undressing, he explained to Ben, "When a hunter seeks moose, caribou, sheep, goat, deer, or a black bear, he should fast and bathe to purify himself because they are *Dikaankaawu*'s favorite animals. For fish, rabbits, and birds, He does not require a fast or a bath, only a promise that nothing will be wasted. But in time of need, I prepare myself with a bath."

"Does it work, Grandpa?"

"Yes, *Dikaankaawu* has sent me many animals."

Skepticism in his voice, Ben asked, "How do you know it isn't just a coincidence when you kill an animal after the prayer and bath stuff."

"I know!"

*I'll believe it when I see it, Grandpa.*

Ben grinned when he saw the faded, pinked-tinged long johns. They had been white once, but probably got washed with something red. Taking them off, Grandfather stepped into the lake. Ben shivered thinking about the cold water. Soaping thoroughly, Grandfather bathed and washed his hair. Finally, he dried off and dressed again. "I am ready now, Bennie."

Grandfather faced east, hands out in supplication, and called out, "*Dikaankaawu*, I am coming into your woods to set snares. I will not stay long. But I need food for your children. I will not waste anything."

Clapping his hands four times and raising his voice, Grandfather hollered, "Hootz, we do not mean to disturb you."

Ben remembered as a little boy going berry picking with his grandfather. Mimicking him, he would clap his hands and holler at the bear. He couldn't recall the reason. Something about letting God know what you are up to. Then he would let you use his woods and animals. And they always let Hootz, the grizzly bear, know too.

After the prayer, Ben followed Grandfather across the river and along a game trail that led down the valley. The old man stopped at a growth of willows close to the camp. "Let's see what we can find in here. Rabbits like willow thickets." He examined the ground. "Ah, here we are, rabbit droppings." He picked up several round, black pellets. "Not a lot of sign around here, but we'll try some snares, anyway."

Grandfather cut a limb from a lodgepole pine and trimmed all the branches off. Next, he sharpened one end and drove the piece into the ground at an angle. He retrieved the fishing reel from his jacket, cut off a two-foot length of line and made a slipknot loop in one end. The other end he tied to the slanting stick. Then he adjusted the loop until it hung in the center of the trail.

"Bennie, I use my fist to measure from the ground to the bottom of the loop. This gives you about four inches—just right for rabbit. Here's how it works: when the rabbit's head or body hits the noose, the slip knot slides down and tightens up. The more the rabbit struggles, the tighter the knot gets. Snares work on ptarmigan too. Set your snares in the willows where they have been feeding."

"Let me give it a try. "

Ben put his hand into the loop and the knot slid down. "That really works." Impressed, he asked, "How do you know all this stuff? I've never seen rabbits around Wrangell."

"In my younger days, I lived in Telegraph Creek. Lots of rabbits there. I cut wood for the steamboats on the Stikine and trapped during the winter. That's where I met your grandmother. She wanted to live in Wrangell. Didn't like the cold winters in Canada."

Cutting off a piece of fishing line, Grandfather handed it to Ben. "Now, it's your turn, Bennie." He supervised the setting of a dozen snares. The snares had to work perfectly before he gave his approval.

"Bennie, there's not a lot of rabbit sign here. But this is moose, sheep, goat, caribou, and maybe deer country. We won't go hungry."

"Sounds good, Grandpa, but we don't have a rifle. How are we going to do it?"

"The way our ancestors did it. Our people hunted for thousands of years before the white man came. As a boy, I hunted with a bow. We were poor and didn't have money for cartridges. I'll teach you the old ways,"

Grandfather said, proud of his people.

Ben thought, *I don't know. With a rifle, we might have a chance. Wishful thinking, Grandpa, wishful thinking.*

Trying to sound supportive, Ben said, "I'm pretty handy with tools. Took all the shop classes I could. Made all A's."

"Bennie," Grandfather assured him, "I will show you how to make bows and spears that will kill anything in this country."

As they walked on, Ben worked it over in his mind again, but was still unconvinced they could survive without a rifle. Rounding a bend in the trail, Grandfather stopped. Ben nearly ran into him.

Startled, a grizzly reared up on its hind legs. Fifty feet up the trail stood the biggest animal Ben had ever seen outside a zoo.

# CHAPTER 8

Ben wanted to run, but his legs wouldn't move. His body refused to obey his brain. Cold fear surged through him. The encounter seemed unreal, like a movie scene played in slow motion. Ben's throat and chest tightened as his body prepared him for flight.

Grandfather studied the grizzly. "We're downwind," he whispered, "The bear can't smell us, and he can't make us out. Stay put."

The bear turned his head toward them and sniffed the air to identify the threat. Dropping down, muscles rippling under the grey hide, swinging and jerking his head, the grizzly warned the intruders they were in his territory .

"Don't make a sound," Grandfather whispered. Ben barely shook his head, watching the bear in fearful fascination. Pacing back and forth and looking around, the bear reared up again testing the air. Moaning and growling, he lowered his head and walked up the trail.

Ben breathed a sigh of relief. The bear was leaving.

Suddenly the grizzly turned and looked in their direction again, huffing and snorting.

In a low, hard voice, Grandfather told Ben, "I want you up a tree, now!"

"No," Ben refused, in a hoarse whisper. "I won't go unless you do."

Hootz watched them. Clacking his teeth and slobbering, the bear reared up, stomping the ground with his front legs.

"He's getting ready to come at us."

Sucking in his breath, Ben braced himself.

Striding forward toward the bear, Grandfather shouted, "Hootz, we mean you no harm." The grizzly swung his head. Then, in a stiff-legged walk, the bear came down the trail and stopped ten feet from Grandfather. Eyes set in a large dished-out face, slobber hanging from his jaws, the grizzly studied Grandfather. Careful not to look in into the bear's eyes, Grandfather spoke softly and respectfully in Tlingit, "Hootz, I am Danewak of the Yehl Kit people, house of Yehl Kudi. We do not mean to trespass in your territory." Grandfather held out his hands to show he had no weapons. "We will go in peace."

Petrified with fear, Ben felt the hair rising on the back of his neck. Through terrified eyes, he watched the bear. The grey colored grizzly stood on all fours, his front legs bowed in, each foot armed with six inches of black claws.

Moving around Grandfather, the bear stopped next to Ben.

Ben felt the grizzly's eyes on him. He lowered his own and tried not to breath. He could smell the rank, mustiness of the animal. He could hear the bear breathing. His pulse beat in his ears.

He waited.

With a low, menacing growl, the grizzly ambled away, back up the trail to where he had been digging marmots minutes before. He turned and looked back at them, then disappeared into the bush.

"Bennie," Grandfather whispered, "He's gone for now. But we haven't seen the last of him."

Gulping air, Ben stumbled down the trail on rubbery legs. His knees didn't want to hold him up. *Please God don't let me fall.* The power, the danger, and the anger of the grizzly hung over the trail like something alive.

As they eased around a bend in the trail, Grandfather cautioned Ben, "Easy . . . don't run! You can't outrun a bear. Hootz could come back anytime. If he attacks, get on your belly hug the ground with your hands behind your neck. Play dead. If you have to, fight back—go for the eyes and nose," he said, watching the back trail.

As soon as they hit camp, Ben felt a surge relief and joy. Grandfather built up the fire. The dry wood burst into flames, sending a shower of sparks into the air. Heart still pounding, Ben dropped down on a boulder next to the fire, reliving the encounter. "I was scared spitless. Couldn't move."

Pouring a cup of hot tea, Grandfather handed it to Ben. "Here, this will make you feel better. You would be a fool not to be scared. He scared me, too. Bigger than I figured. Standing up, he's a good ten feet. Probably weighs near a thousand pounds. Big animal for this country. I knew he was coming for us when he started swinging his head and hitting the ground with his front legs."

"That was pretty brave thing you did Grandpa, talking to the bear. I thought we were dead. He was so close I could smell him. *It's little hard to believe that a bear understands Tlingit, Grandpa. I just don't go for that old Indian stuff. But it worked.*

"I got most of what you told him, but the Tlingit sounded different."

"Formal Tlingit, Bennie to show respect. I reminded Hootz that his tribe and the Raven people have been friends for a long time. And I told him I was Silver Eyes of the Raven Clan, Raven's Nest House, and that you were of the Wolf Clan of Wolf Den House. He let us go, but I felt his spirit—it was dark and angry. He means us harm, Bennie."

Ben felt goose bumps rise on his neck.

"Anyway, Hootz is gone from around here. "

Ben looked toward the ridge, thinking the bear was crossing over it, but he saw no sign of the animal. "How do you know, Grandpa?"

"See the crows flying at the end of the lake? Any bears around, they'd be diving and making a fuss."

Ben watched the crows skimming along the water. "Yeah, you're right Grandpa. They don't look too concerned about anything."

"You start worrying when they are worried. In the bush, you've got to keep your eyes and ears open. I nearly got us killed today looking for rabbit sign. Should've been paying attention. You don't make too many mistakes with that animal. We'll stay around camp for a couple days. Give Hootz a chance to move on."

"I'm all for that, Grandpa." Ben looked up the lake, half expecting to see the grizzly charging out of the brush. Relieved, he turned back to the fire and tossed a piece of wood on it.

"It's getting late in the day," said Grandfather. "I'll fix us a little grub. Bennie, rake some coals out and peel some spuds. I'll put the bacon on." Bustling around the fire, he prepared food.

*I know what you are up to Grandpa. Trying to get my mind off the bear. Think a little food will make me feel better? Not going to do it. That bear scared the crap out if me.*

Later, sitting next to the fire with a cup of tea, Ben had to admit he felt better. Grandfather joined him. "You didn't like going to the Wrangell Indian Institute did you, Bennie?"

The question caught Ben by surprise. "What brought that on, Grandpa?"

"Your mom sent you to the Institute to please me. I thought it would be good for you to be with other Indian kids. I'm sorry, Bennie."

"It was O.K., but I didn't fit in. You know what the kids called me?

"Something bad?"

"The *ar shu*."

"They called you half-breed? You should've told me Bennie. I'd have talked to the principal."

"I fight my own battles, Grandpa. The Institute had its share of bullies. I was a scrawny kid in fifth grade when I entered there. I had to learn how to fight. I guess they thought a half-breed from Seattle would be a pushover. I wasn't. Some learned the hard way."

Grandfather smiled.

# CHAPTER 9

"Bennie," Grandfather decided, "It's time to look over the valley to see what's down there in the way of food. Snares are not catching anything. We need to find some type of shelter, too. Looks like we're going to be here for awhile. It's up to us to use the country. The bush doesn't allow too many mistakes. We have to live with it."

"Couldn't the bear still be there?" In his mind's eye, Ben could see the grizzly standing in the trail, popping his teeth, getting ready to come at them. He relived the fear.

"Hard to say. He's had a couple days to move on. Could be anyplace. Grizzlies range for hundreds of miles looking for food. We have to keep our eyes and ears open, particularly with that animal. Never seen one like him before."

*Not what I wanted to hear, Grandpa.* Ben thought. *Not much of a choice. If the bear doesn't kill you, the country will.*

"O.K. which way we going, Bennie?"

"The valley runs north."

"And how do you know?"

"The sun comes up in the east, which is to my right," Ben said pointing. "So, I'm facing north."

"And this river. What does it drain into?"

"The Stikine."

"How do you know?"

"That's what you told me."

"I could be wrong."

*Why all the questions?* Ben thought, irritated.

"No, you're not wrong. The valley slopes downhill to the west. So the river has got to flow that way. What's this all about?" Ben asked frowning.

"It's about depending on yourself. Yes, the river drains into the Stikine."

*Am I missing something, here?*

Puzzled, Ben followed Grandfather. They crossed the river and onto a game trail that meandered in a northerly direction down into the lower valley. When they approached the bend in the trail where they startled the grizzly, Ben's senses alerted. He swept the site with his eyes, checking for the bear and listening for alarm calls. "You're learning Bennie," Grandfather said with satisfaction.

They continued down the valley, Grandfather pointing out edible plants. As they walked along a meadow, they neared a series of shallow ponds. "These places grow some tasty food, Bennie. See the plant with the big, shiny leaves and yellow flowers? That's a water lily. The roots and seeds can be roasted, and the seeds can also be ground into flour. Ponds are also favorite feeding spots for . . . Look!" Grandfather pointed down the trail.

"I don't see anything except ponds and trees," Ben said, afraid he was missing something.

"Look down the trail about fifty feet, near the second pond," Grandfather said, pointing. "See where that dead tree leans out on the edge of the meadow?"

Then Ben saw the ungainly, dark brown animal stepping out of the birches into the meadow. "I see him!" Ben whispered, excited. "He's bigger than a horse. Got pretty big horns. I've never eaten moose before, Grandpa."

"Better than beef. Indians have been eating moose for . . . I don't know how long. Four or five hundred pounds of meat there. The bull is in the velvet now. Come September the horns will harden and he will scrape that spongy cover off."

The old man smiled, "Then he will start courting the ladies. He'll get his share, too. Looks like he's coming our way. If he doesn't wind us, you will get a real close look at him."

Grandfather studied the moose. The animal continued along the edge of the meadow, stopping in a growth of willow directly in front of them. "I could hit him with a rock," Ben whispered.

"He's probably in here to feed, Ben. But something's got him spooked." The old man looked around and listened for alarm calls. "This doesn't look good."

The bull's nostrils flared as he tested the wind. His eyes shifted back and forth, scanning the terrain. Rotating his ears, the bull listened. In a slow, hesitant walk, the moose started across the meadow. He stopped and gazed at the far side of the clearing, opposite Ben and Grandfather. Turning, he looked in their direction.

Grandfather grabbed Ben by the shoulder and whispered, "Ease back into the timber so we can get a little cover. Something's not right, Bennie."

Just as they stepped behind the trees, a grizzly came crashing out of the bush and leaped on the moose's back, the bear's weight collapsing the bull's hindquarters. He sunk his claws into each side of the bull's rib cage. Then the grizzly locked his jaws on the moose's neck and rolled off, pulling the moose down. With a slash of his paw, the bear gutted the bull.

He thrust his muzzle into the cavity and tore out the beating heart. The bull bawled a deep-throated cry of pain and terror, ending in a grunting cough. The grizzly reared, testing the air, then turned and stared in their direction, his muzzle covered with blood and gore. A loop of guts hung from one paw. Dropping back down, the bear buried his head in the moose's stomach, feeding on the entrails.

Grandfather whispered, "Don't move. Bennie."

Ben nodded, unable to speak.

Suddenly, the grizzly stopped feeding. He smelled the air and circled the kill, then reared up to his full height. Ten feet of carnivore stood just outside the trees, his muzzle and head covered with blood. Raising his forelegs, the silver-tip exposed his claws. Ears laid back, swinging his head, the bear watched the edge of the timber where Ben and Grandfather were hiding.

"Easy, Bennie," Grandfather whispered. He tightened his grip on Ben's shoulder. "Don't move."

Dropping down, the bear plunged his head into the stomach cavity and ripped out the liver. Holding it down with a paw, he tore at the still warm organ. Suddenly, he turned a bloody muzzle toward the woods again, and erupted into a charge, muscles flowed under the shaggy hide like steel cables. A thousand pounds of bear, armed with teeth and claws, came at them in ground-eating bounds.

*We're not going to walk away this time, Grandpa.*

# CHAPTER 10

Skidding to a stop directly in front of them, the grizzly turned and charged along the edge of the brush. Frantically dodging and running for cover, a red fox dove into an opening in the rocks. The bear sniffed the hole for a minute, then gave up and raced back to the kill. He scattered the jays and ravens, and returned to tearing out chunks of meat.

"He's busy feeding. It's time to get ourselves back into the timber. Slow now. Slow. We're downwind. He can't smell us. Let's get out of here."

Body still pumping adrenalin, Ben followed Grandfather. He stopped several times to look back. Wetting a finger, he tested the wind. "We're still downwind from him. You can't be too careful. Let's go, Bennie."

"That's the same bear, isn't it Grandpa?" Ben asked.

"The same one, Bennie. This is his territory."

When they entered camp, Grandfather threw wood on the fire and put water on for tea. Ben huddled around the blaze reliving the grizzly encounter. *I thought we were dead.*

Grandfather handed him a cup. "Nothing like good, hot tea, Bennie."

"Grandpa! Tea doesn't fix everything," Ben said, irritated.

"No, it doesn't Bennie. But I made it extra strong and sweet. It'll give you a little jolt. Enjoy it. If that bear had gone another ten feet, we wouldn't be drinking tea... or doing anything else for that matter. We'd be listening for the shaman's drum and . . ."

"The shaman's drum?" Ben interrupted. "Oh, I remember that old story. He picks you up and takes you to Heaven in a big boat . . . or something like that?"

Grandfather shrugged. "Something like that."

*Grandpa, Grandpa, Grandpa. The boat is just a myth. But that bear is real. Didn't they teach you anything when you went to school in Sitka? Jeez!*

"Well, I'll fix us some grub," said Grandfather. He cooked bacon, potatoes and two eggs and handed Ben a plate. "Enjoy! This is the last of the eggs and potatoes."

"Aren't you going to eat?" Ben asked.

"I'll eat later." He finished his tea and handed the cup to Ben. "Right now I'm going to bed. Tomorrow we should look for a permanent camp of some kind. Lot of cliffs along the river. Might find a cave or overhang we can use, or build a lean-to."

Ben looked at his watch. "It's pretty early Grandpa, only 7:30."

"Not for tired old men, Bennie."

*That's not like you, Grandpa. You don't look well.* Ben covered him with spruce boughs and built up the fire.

The warmth and safety of the fire brought back nostalgic images of the first fish camp Ben went to with Grandfather when he was a little kid. A place of fun. People laughing, joking, playing tricks on each other, telling the old stories. Someone picking on a guitar. He didn't understand why several women kept watch over the older boys and girls and wouldn't let them go into the woods alone.

*Now I know*, Ben thought, smiling at the memory of couples being marched out of the woods by some elderly lady.

An Elder wearing a crest hat with four cylinders and a Chilkat blanket, symbols of his high rank in the tribe, stood up in the crowd. A sudden hush fell over the crowd. In formal Tlingit, the Elder blessed the gathering of the clan. The Elder then threw parts of salmon into the stream. When Ben asked Grandfather why, he told him no one remembered exactly. Just that it was always done on the first night.

Then the chatter started again. The cooks grilled red salmon fillets over an alder wood fire. Rich odors of fresh coffee, fry bread, and salmon filled the air. The Coho salmon had come up the stream again and the smoking racks would be full. *Dikaankaawu* had heard their prayers.

Grandfather coughed, pulling Ben out of his memories. *That was then, this is now*, he thought. Ben didn't sleep at all that night because of his worrying about Grandfather. Whenever he checked on the old man he seemed restless, mumbling in Tlingit.

At first light, Ben got up for good. *I'm going to let you sleep*, he thought, looking at Grandfather, who was finally resting peacefully. Ben threw wood on the fire and walked down to the lake to get water for tea. Out on the water a loon fluted, an unearthly-scream. Ben shivered.

Hearing a cough, Ben turned back to camp. Grandfather was sitting up.

"How do you feel, Grandpa?"

"Didn't get much sleep last night. Just getting old. Once I start moving around. I'll be fine."

Ben handed him a cup of tea. "I'll heat up the food," he said, setting the frying pan on the fire.

"I'm not hungry, Bennie. Later, I'll cook us up a good feed. You go ahead and eat."

"I'm not hungry either," Ben said, pulling the frying pan off the coals. Worrying about his grandfather had killed his appetite.

After a few minutes Grandfather laid down again. "I'm still tired, Bennie. I need a little more sleep. Would you cover me up? Little cold last night."

"Sure, Grandpa." Ben said, arranging boughs over him.

Grandfather woke up late in the day. Ben helped him to a seat on a boulder next to the fire. "I'm going to get you some tea." Ben poured a cup and sipped it to see how hot it was and held the cup while the old man drank. For a while, the tea seemed to revive him, but he soon dozed off again.

Afraid he would fall off the rock, Ben said, "I think you need to go back to bed, Grandpa." Ben helped him onto the pine boughs and covered him up.

"I'm cold, Bennie. Tell Grandma to get a blanket."

"Grandmother isn't here," Ben said gently, "I'll build up the fire."

# CHAPTER 11

Once again, Ben stayed up most of the night watching over Grandfather and feeding the fire. Falling into a half-sleep, he awoke in the cold of early morning. Hearing his grandfather moan, Ben jumped up to check on him. "Grandpa! Grandpa! What's the matter?"

Grandfather's voice came so low and weak that Ben had to lean down to hear him. "Benjamin, Last night, the owl called my name."

"The owl?" Then Ben remembered. The death owl! "Grandpa, that's just a legend. You're not going to die."

The old man smiled, his mind wandering to days past. "Very pretty. She had laughing eyes." Mumbling something in Tlingit, he tried to rise.

"My song."

"Song? What song? I don't understand," Ben asked, puzzled.

"My death song."

It dawned on Ben what Grandfather wanted. Some of the old people believed that the Great Canoe came only for those who sang their death song. Panicky, Ben said, "Grandpa, you don't need a death song. You're not going to die. You're just tired."

"I am *Danawag*. Silver Eyes of the Yehl Kudi."

Grandfather searched the sky. "*Kaa Shageinyaa, Kaa Shageinyaa* is waiting. The *Kaagwaanton* People are coming."

Ben had only a vague idea what Grandfather was talking about. Something about the clan and the Place Above. Grandfather thrashed around trying to get up. "No Grandpa. You'll hurt yourself!" Gently, Ben restrained him.

"Help me up, Bennie," he said in a stronger voice.

Frightened, Ben lifted Grandfather under the arms and helped him up. Facing east and stretching out his arms, the old man began his death chant. In his mind, Ben translated the song. He couldn't explain how he could understand the ancient words.

Xagax ax du hunxw

*I am sorry my brother*

Yen wae naadi

*When you go*

Xat kuch chratsch Wa.e tsug

*I will see you again*

Hagu qoxde ax du hunxw

*Come back my brother*

Naxawe kaa yakghel yau

*From the spirit land*

Hagu qoxde

*Come back*

Grandfather's voice trailed off.

Fear seized Ben. "Grandpa! Grandpa! Don't leave me!"

Gazing into the sky, Grandfather said, "See the Great War Canoe? It brings the *Kaagwaanton* People. The shaman is standing in the bow, beating the drum. Do you hear the drum? The singing?"

Ben sobbed, "No, Grandpa." Then he heard the solemn, unchanging beat that seemed to come out of the earth itself. It filled Ben's very being. "I don't understand. It can't be real. What's going on?" Frantically, he looked around for the source of the drums and the singing. The singing was in Tlingit, but a kind he had never heard before. He wasn't hearing it with his ears, but with his mind.

Ben looked at Grandfather. Transfixed, the old man stared at the sky. Abruptly, the drums and singing stopped. Grandfather gasped and fell back. Ben caught him and eased him down on the bed where he lay on his back as if asleep, white hair framing his strong face.

Gently, Ben shook him. "Wake up, Grandpa. Wake up!" Ben pleaded, tears welling up. "Wake up! Don't die! You're asleep, aren't you Grandpa? Oh God, wake up!" But Grandfather didn't wake up. He was gone.

For hours after Grandfather's death, Ben sat on the rock next to the fire, his brain locked in disbelief. Finally, he threw wood on the fire and curled up next to it.

He dreamt he was safe in his own bed, the Hudson Bay wool blanket pulled up around him. The same brightly striped one that Dad slept under as a boy. Shadow the cat curled up at his feet. He was snuggled between Mom and Dad, safe and warm. But then Dad got up. Ben couldn't find him. He ran after him, but the train was too fast. Ben couldn't catch it.

Heart beating, gasping for breath, Ben woke up confused and disorientated. "Why am I sleeping on the ground? Mom! Where's my blanket?" Struggling to stand up, he stared at the lake. Then he dropped back down on the boulder. *I thought I was home.* Nothing seemed real to him. He couldn't accept Grandfather's death.

The next morning, Ben forced himself to prepare a grave. Everything was unreal. Ben felt detached like he was watching someone else. He selected a spot near a birch tree growing next to a boulder. The site was just a few feet outside the camp. Because Grandfather was a big man, Ben couldn't move him too far. Ben marked off a six-foot space for a grave. With a flat rock, he scraped out the dirt and debris until he hit solid rock when he was waist deep in the hole. The digging took him all morning. Next, he lined the grave with fresh-cut fir boughs. Then he removed Grandfather's pocket watch and wallet, along with his jacket, and laid them aside.

Lifting Grandfather by the shoulders, Ben dragged him to the grave and gently placed him in it. Ben then arranged Grandfather into a sleeping position, brushed the sand out of his hair and looked at him for the last time. Gathering flat rocks, Ben covered the grave.

Just above the beach line, Ben picked several armloads of flowers in red, yellow, purple, pink, and white. They grew in wild profusion under the long hours of June sunlight. He recognized a few: fireweed, wild roses, and lupine. They grew in Wrangell, too.

Ben arranged the flowers around the grave, then he stepped back and looked at his work. "It looks nice, Grandpa. The white birch tree is kinda like a like a cross. And this is a pretty spot. From here you can look down the valley, not too far from where we were fishing."

Ben thought for a minute. He felt like there should be some kind of funeral. "I don't know how it was done in the old days, but if I get out of here I'll see you have a proper one. For now, this will have to do." With the pointed handle of the file, Ben scratched on a flat rock:

Cyrus Paul

Danawag Yehl

1870 - 1950

"I'm not sure of your birth date or the spelling of your Tlingit name and clan, but it's the best I can do."

Ben sat next to the grave, rearranging the flowers. Speaking softly, he said, "Grandpa, I'm glad for the time we had together. You were like a father to me. I hope you are with Grandma now. Good-bye. I love you."

Back at the fire, Ben ate the rest of the cold bacon, an egg, and potatoes from the frying pan. It was the last meal Grandfather cooked. He ate without tasting the food—the joy of campfire cooking died with grandfather. Ben felt an emptiness food couldn't fill.

He picked up Grandfather's jacket. The faded, forest-green garment smelled of smoke, the bush, and Grandfather. Ben huddled next to the fire wearing the jacket, and fell into a dreamless sleep.

# CHAPTER

After Grandfather's death, Ben spent his days searching the sky for a rescue plane and wandering aimlessly back and forth along the lake shore. He lost track of time. The deep hopelessness of the situation pressed on his chest like a vise. Fear of the grizzly kept Ben near camp. When he left the safety of the fire to check the snares, his body tensed with fear. His traps produced only one rabbit. The rest of the time he lived on fish, until they started feeding on some kind of insect and refused Ben's lure. Except for a little tea, he soon ran out of food.

Ben could still feel Grandfather's presence in camp. One morning Ben looked at Grandfather's boots, still standing neatly by the bed just as he left them. He picked up Grandfather's jacket and pressed it to his face. The smell of his grandfather brought more tears to his eyes.

"I can't stay here anymore. It's time to leave."

Saddened by the task, Ben finally unpacked Dan's army pack. *Sorry I have to get into your stuff, but I need the packsack.* He hung the waders by the feet in a tree. *I hope you get to use these again.* He stood for a minute thinking of the pilot. *Hope you make it out, Dan.*

Once the pack was empty, Ben began filling it with the things he would need. First, he arranged Grandfather's boots, the frying pan, coffee pot, and Dan's saw at the bottom of the pack. Then he added three tin cups, three tin plates, a butcher knife, and eating utensils. He was only going to take two table knives, but then he remembered Grandfather talking about using them to make arrowheads, so he brought them all. Next, he put in the first-aid kit, the sewing kit, the shaving mirror, a bar of soap, two cans of tobacco and a pipe, Dan's creel and tackle box, the near-empty sack of sugar, a box of salt, and a box of pepper. Along the side of the pack, Ben made room for three fishing rods and reels. He attached Grandfather's hunting knife to his belt and stuck the sharpening stone in his pocket. When he picked up Grandfather's jacket, he choked up. Ben folded it with care and placed it in the top of the pack.

Ben walked over to the grave to say good-bye. "Grandpa, I just can't stay here any longer. Too much sadness. You knew you were dying, didn't you? That's the reason you showed me all that survival stuff and made sure I knew where North was. Well, I'm heading that way. I've got to find some food and a better place to stay."

"I'm glad you and Mom made up. And I loved spending summers with you. The fish camps and hunting trips were great. No one could smoke salmon like you." Ben laughed as he remembered. "I promise I'll come back for a visit. I love you."

Hungry, alone, and dwarfed by the wilderness, Ben shouldered the pack and started down the valley. He followed a game trail that snaked along the cliff-side of the river. As Ben approached the moose-kill site, his body tensed. The image of the grizzly killing the moose was still sharp in his mind. Ben scanned the area and listened for alarm cries from the birds, but he heard nothing. He picked up his pace, frequently looking back over his shoulder, until he was well away.

As Ben walked, he searched the cliffs for a cave or an over-hanging ledge. He found several good places for a temporary camp, but nothing that would work for a long stay. There was no doubt in Ben's mind about that he would be out here on his own over the winter . . . *if* he lasted that long.

Tired and discouraged, he plodded down the valley. Late in the day, the trail climbed up thirty feet through the willows and heavy brush onto a flat, sandy, park-like strip of land between the river and cliffs. Stands of cottonwood trees and clumps of evergreens opened up to grassy meadows. Heavy stands of lodgepole pines and birch followed the edge of the cliffs, skirting rock debris.

Up ahead, crows quarreled over something near a cottonwood tree. *Hope you got it right, Grandpa, about bears and crows.* Ben shrugged off his pack, "Well kid, I guess this is as good a place to camp as any."

While collecting wood for a fire, Ben noticed a game trail leading through a dense stand of birch growing along the edge of the cliff. Curious, he followed the trail through the trees. It came out into a natural clearing near the base of the cliffs. Ben couldn't believe his eyes.

A cave!

Ben ran over to inspect it. Cautiously, he edged toward the opening. Not knowing what he might find, he tossed rocks into the entrance. Once he was satisfied that nothing lurked inside, Ben crept into the dark cave. Weak sunlight filtered through a hole near the back.

He stood in the entrance until his eyes adjusted. The low, oval-shaped interior ended in a pile of rubble at the back. It was hard to tell in the dark, but it looked plenty big. Maybe this would work!

"First thing I'm going to do is get a fire going and cheer this place up." Excited by his find, Ben raced back down the trail and retrieved his packsack and axe.

Along the cliffs he found a stand of lodgepole pine killed by a rockslide. He selected a yellow-streaked trunk and cut it into sections. The chopping sound echoed loudly against the cliffs and seemed to carry a long way. Ben stopped several times to check the ridge for the grizzly. He finished quickly and dragged the sections to the cave.

Ben split a log into kindling and used one piece to whittle into shavings. From the rubble in back of the cave, he picked out rocks and built a rough fireplace. Then he laid a fire and touched a match to the shavings. They flared up into the resin-streaked wood and burst into flame, snapping and shooting sparks.

The firelight revealed a dark stain on the grey granite wall. At the bottom of the wall, Ben noticed a pile of rocks. First, he thought it was natural, then he had a sudden realization. "Hey! That's an old fire pit, just like mine. And that stain is from the smoke. Wow! People actually lived here." But even Ben could tell it had been a long, long time ago. "My fire could be the first one here for hundreds of years."

Touching the stain, Ben wondered about the people whose fires recorded their presence. *Who were they? What happened to them?* Somehow he didn't feel so alone. In his mind's eye, Ben could see people sitting around a long-ago fire. He felt a kinship with the ancient people.

Ben was brought back to the present when hunger gnawed at his belly. "All I've got left is a little tea," he muttered. Still, it was better than nothing, so he dug the coffee pot out of the packsack and went down to the river to get water. There, fish were rising, making little bubble circles as they came to the surface.

*Maybe they're feeding,* Ben thought as he raced back to the cave. Returning with his rod, he stood on the riverbank catching his breath and anxiously searching the water to see if the fish were still feeding. Bubble circles dotted the water. Relieved, Ben got ready to cast.

Then he hesitated, thinking of Grandfather and the old ways. Ben closed his eyes and quickly mumbled the fish prayer he'd heard Grandfather say: "I will not waste anything." He cast his lure into the water where the river eddied around a boulder, then twitched the rod and began to reel in. Immediately the rod bent and a grayling exploded out of the water. Ben didn't play the fish. He was too hungry. Instead he reeled it in, killed it, and quickly caught two more. Abruptly, the fish stopped biting.

Ben roasted the grayling over the coals of his fire in the cave and ate all three in big, hungry gulps. For the first time since Grandfather's death, Ben felt like he had a chance.

*Maybe I can make it.*

His stomach full, Ben felt hope for the first time since the crash. Ben inspected the cave. "If the roof was any lower I'd have to duck. The walls are pretty close here, too, but that's good. The roof and sloping walls will reflect the heat. I'll clean out a place for my bed across from the fire. It'll work out great!" He joked to himself, "I'll be able to throw wood on the fire without even getting out of bed."

Next, he checked the back of the cave. There it widened out with a higher roof. "Plenty of room back here." Looking up, Ben could see the hole where the light came in. He climbed up the rock debris to see what was up there, if anything. "Looks like part of the roof caved in. Long time ago."

Full of hope, Ben stepped outside to look over the cliff. The cave had formed at the base, the roughly dome-shaped opening set back under an overhang. On one side of the opening, two large birches had taken root. "I'll have to close up some of that entrance," Ben said, thinking about the grizzly. "I only need a couple of feet to get in." Ten feet above the opening, a slab of rock rested against the side of the cliff. He sized it up. "Looks a little spooky to me. Might fall. I'll check it out later."

"But right now, I need to do a little clean-up for my bed." Ben went back inside and with a flat rock began raking out porcupine quills and rodent droppings. He picked up a long silver-grey hair and sniffed it. It had a rank smell; the smell of danger. He held it up to the light. "This didn't come from any little critter. It's gotta be a bear. Hope it's not that grizzly. That's all I need." Instinctively, he turned and looked at the doorway, but there was nothing there.

Once the floor was cleaned, Ben made a spruce bough mattress for his bed. He tied more boughs together with fishing line to make a blanket. Ben tried the bed. "Not bad. Keep a good fire going and I'll be warm."

Something on the ground next to the new bed shined in the firelight; something Ben had missed in his clean-up. A spearhead. Delighted, he picked it up and examined it, tracing its finely chipped edge with his finger. *It's like touching someone from the past.*

Ben carefully placed the point on a natural shelf that ran along the wall above the fire pit. He felt a bond with the ancient hunter: *If you made it, maybe I can too.*

# CHAPTER 13

Early the next morning, Ben woke up cold and hungry. Shivering, he got up to stoke the fire, but the ashes were cold. "What a screw-up! I should've gotten up last night to throw some wood on the fire." Scraping away the ashes, he shredded birch bark tinder and laid kindling around it. But he couldn't find the matches.

"I'm sure I put them on that rock." He checked his shirt pocket, but his finger's probed empty space. Frantically, he searched all his pockets. Then he raked through the debris he'd cleaned out of the cave. "I couldn't lose the matches. I just used them yesterday. How could I be so careless? Dumb! Dumb! Dumb!"

Ben saw something green on the floor near the back of the cave and raced over. "Matches!" Relief flooded through him. But when he opened the cover, he couldn't believe his eyes. The match heads had been chewed off. The cover was still readable though: *Wrangell Saloon. Where good friends meet.*

"Couldn't you have chewed off the cover and let the matches alone, you lousy little pea brain?" Ben wadded up the cover and slammed it to the floor. "If I ever catch you, whatever you are, you're gonna be history!"

Stalking back to the fire pit, Ben looked at the dead ashes. "I can't make it without fire." Panic numbed him. "Why didn't I wake up and throw wood on the fire? Gotta think," he told himself, searching his mind for an answer.

"In the Scouts, we made fire with flint and steel. Indians must've found flint for the spearhead somewhere around here. Gotta be something that'll spark." Ben searched the cliff face for flint, breaking different kinds of rocks to see if they would spark. He spent the whole day testing rocks. Some gave off weak sparks, but he knew those wouldn't light a fire.

That night he went without a fire. He wore Grandfather's coat and pulled the spruce blanket around him, but he still felt the cold. Fear of the bear kept him in a half-sleep. The next morning he got up, cold, hungry and groggy from lack of sleep.

Discouraged, Ben searched again for flint. He had gone only a short distance up the valley, when a dark glacier-scarred boulder caught his eye. With the back of the hunting knife, Ben struck the rock. Every blow sent up a shower of sparks.

Breaking off a piece with another rock, Ben raced back to the cave and prepared a handful of paper-thin birch bark for tinder by cutting it into long pieces and wadding it up into a ball like Grandfather had shown him. Striking the rock with the knife, sent a shower of sparks into the tinder. But the bark wouldn't light. He tried again; still the tinder wouldn't ignite.

"Maybe it's not fine enough." He pounded the dry bark with a rock into a fluffy wad and tried again. Still, it wouldn't ignite. Ben mulled the problem over in his mind. "In the Scouts we used charred cloth to catch the spark," he thought aloud. An idea formed.

Ben grabbed a coal from the fire pit and pulverized it into a fine powder with a rock. He dabbed the tinder into the powder, covering it with a coating of charcoal. "This has gotta work." He breathed a silent prayer.

Striking the flint, Ben sent a shower of sparks into the tinder. Glowing red spots appeared. He blew too hard. The spots flickered out. He struck the flint again, sparks shot into the tinder. Blowing gently, Ben nursed the spots until they spread and broke into bluish-orange flames.

He touched the flame to the tinder. It caught, igniting the pitchy wood. "I did it!" he shouted, the cave magnifying the sound. Startled by the noise, he said softly, "Grandfather, you would be proud of me."

Ben started down to the river to get water when a porcupine waddled in front of him. Sensing danger, the animal broke into an awkward, tail-slapping, quills-erect, teeth-chattering run. After a short chase, Ben killed the animal with an axe blow. Out of breath from the excitement, Ben promised, "I won't waste a morsel."

Ben inspected the porcupine. "How do I clean this thing without getting stuck full of quills?" With a stick, he turned the porcupine over on its back. No quills on the belly. "It's gotta be done from here." Ben had never cleaned an animal before, but he had watched Grandfather butcher and skin deer plenty of times.

Grandfather's knife was still razor sharp. Inserting the point of the knife at the base of the tail, Ben tried a few tentative jabs. The blade easily pierced the flesh. He slit the belly up the center. The guts rolled out in white loops and he cut them free. "So far so good."

Then Ben made a cut up the center of each back leg and started cutting the hide free of the body. Working carefully, he skinned out the porcupine. He made the last cut around the neck, and lifted the body out of the hide. "Man," Ben gloated, "This is twice the size of a rabbit. Must weigh ten pounds at least!"

Anxious to try the meat, Ben ran into the cave to cook it. At the fire pit, he stopped short. "I don't know how to cook this thing." He had seen pictures of animals hanging over the fire. *Would that work?*

Ben sharpened the end of a stick and pushed it through the animal. Then he stacked rocks on each side of the fire pit and laid the meat over the coals. Soon the cave filled with cooking odors. Meat drippings flared up as they hit the hot coals. Ben waited for what seemed like an eternity for the porcupine to cook. Before it was completely ready, his patience ran out. He had to try it.

The meat tasted like a spruce tree smelled, but to Ben it didn't matter. It was his first kill. As he sat next to the fire, sipping the last of the tea and filling his belly with half-cooked porcupine, Ben felt a rush of confidence.

"I might just make it," he said to the empty cave. The distant hunting cry of a wolf pack broke the silence.

The next morning, Ben left the cave eating a piece of re-cooked porcupine. Tossing the bone away, he wiped his hands on his Levis. "I'm going to look this country over to see what's out here."

Ben climbed up along edge of the cliff, through the birches, and came out above his cave where he had an unobstructed view of the country. "This is will be my lookout. Might give me an edge on that bear."

Ben gazed north at the far horizon. Snow-capped mountains dominated the land. "Grandfather said the Alaska Highway is to the north. If I'm going to get out of here, it won't be that way."

He studied the far end of the valley. It looked like a river flowed along the base of the canyon. "That river has gotta to flow west into the Stikine." Ben looked at his side of the river. Rugged cliffs defined the edge of the valley, with small canyons cutting into the walls. Trees grew along the edges and on the slopes. He recognized birch, their white trunks stood out among the evergreens.

Turning, he checked the other side of the river. There the valley gave away to meadows and sandy flats. Pothole lakes glistened in the sun. Willows edged the waterways forming a mosaic of yellow-green borders. Timbered benches and ridges formed behind the meadows. "Looks like that side might have more game. That's the kind of country where we saw the moose and the grizzly. And Grandfather said rabbits like willows." He felt good hearing a voice, even his own. Ben made mental notes of the lay of the land.

Ben walked to the opening in the cave roof and peered down into the interior. He stamped his foot. "Looks pretty solid. Nothing is going to fall in on me." He then walked down the slope and inspected the huge granite slab hanging over his doorway. It was covered with lichens. "Not much holding this, but it looks like it's been hanging here a long time. Probably O.K." Ben climbed down and returned to the cave.

"Now I've gotta see what's around here to eat. Maybe another porcupine." As Ben stripped line off the fishing reel for snares, he looked out at the country across the river and listened for alarm calls. Cautiously, he walked along the bank until he found a spot where the river flowed around four large boulders. Jumping from rock to rock, he crossed to the other side. A series of flat-topped ridges paralleled the river. Grandfather called them benches.

In the willows at the edge of the river, Ben looked for likely places to set snares. "Maybe I'm missing something, but I don't see much in the way of tracks or droppings." He set snares in the most likely looking places, grateful Grandfather had showed him how. At some sets, Ben built brush "fences" to lead the rabbit into the snare.

Late in the morning, Ben started back to the cave. As he crossed the river, he saw the grizzly's tracks, the deformed paw clearly outlined in the mud. Gagging fear rose in his throat. Ben made a wild run for the cave.

"Stop!" he told himself. "Calm down. You could run into that bear and get yourself killed." Breathing hard Ben stopped, checked the ridge bluffs for movement and listened for birds. Ducks quacked and muttered on the river, but no other sound broke the wilderness silence. Cautiously, Ben returned to the tracks and compared them with his own. The grizzly's tracks were not as sharply defined as his. The edges had crumbled over. "They're not fresh. Maybe a couple days old. But the bear could still be around."

Ben turned and strode quickly back towards the cave, alert to every sound and movement. As soon as he entered the cave, he built-up the fire. Next to the blaze he felt safe. But not knowing where the grizzly was preyed on his mind.

*That animal was just minutes away from finding this place.*

# CHAPTER 14

**As the days passed, Ben** wasn't sure how long he had been in the bush. On the wall, he had kept a rough calendar made with charcoal. Sometimes he forgot to mark off a day. He looked at the calendar, counting twenty marks. "We left Wrangell June fifteenth. That means it must be sometime in July now . . . not that it matters. Sure seems a lot longer."

Ben hadn't eaten regularly since Grandfather died. He survived on fish mostly, with an occasional rabbit and grouse. Small game was scarce, particularly rabbits. He had seen a large cat-like animal that he thought was a lynx. Grandfather said they preyed on rabbits and would clean out an area. Many days he had nothing to eat.

"Well," Ben said to himself, hungry to hear a human voice. "According to Grandpa, I'll need red meat to get through the winter. And since it looks like I'm not getting out of here any time soon, I better make a weapon that'll kill moose and caribou. Grandfather talked about making a bow."

"I haven't fooled around with bow and arrows since I was at the Institute. But this *ar shu* should be able to make one. What kind of wood should I use? When we were kids, we made bows out of willow. Willow is pretty springy."

Down at the river, Ben cut and trimmed several willow saplings. He worked most of the morning shaping the willow with the axe and hunting knife. He discarded the first bow. He had been too eager with the axe and took out too much stock. The second bow, however, shaped up well and felt good in his hands. Aiming the bow, he shot an imaginary moose in the heart.

Puzzling over what to use for a string, Ben's eyes fell on Grandfather's boots. They reached nearly to the knee and had new leather laces. "Perfect." Notching the ends of the bow with his knife, he attached the lace. Testing the bow, Ben shook his head in disappointment. "Pretty weak pull. Maybe O.K. for rabbits and kids playing cowboys and Indians, but not good enough for moose."

The next morning the fish were rising. Ben took two with a spinner. He could have caught more, but two was enough. As he cleaned the fish, Ben muttered, "I'm eating so many fish I'm growing fins. I could use a thick T-bone."

Ben mulled over in his mind what to use for a really strong bow. "Birch might work. Indians used it for lots of things." From the stand of dead birch, Ben selected two straight, small diameter trees. With the saw, he cut the birches into six-foot sections and carried them to the cave.

He worked on the birch bow for most of the day. Pleased with how well it shaped up, Ben fitted the boot lace to the bow and tested it. He felt a constant, heavy resistance as he drew the bow back. "Hey! You've got talent, Ben." But just as he reached the full pull, the bow snapped, one piece striking him across the face. Ben slammed the broken bow to the ground.

Stalking down to the river to cool off, Ben looked at his reflection. A red welt ran across his forehead. Ben scooped up the cool water and splashed his face. Head still hurting, he returned to the cave and examined the faulty bow. It had broken at a knot. "What a birdbrain using a piece with a knot in it! I could've lost an eye."

Ben selected a second piece and this time checked it carefully for defects. Finding none, he began the tedious job of shaping the birch again. This time went much faster. Working on the other bows, he had learned the cutting and scraping techniques. Late in the evening, Ben tested the new bow. This one had a strong steady pull. "Not too shabby."

The next day, Ben cut a bundle of straight, small diameter, willow limbs and shaped them into arrow shafts with his knife. He had read somewhere Indians fire-hardened the tips of their arrows to kill small game. Holding one of the shafts over the fire until it charred the end. Ben then sharpened the tip on a rock. It worked. He ran his fingers over the point. "Not for big game. I really need some kind of arrowhead."

Recalling what Grandfather said about making arrowheads, Ben took out one of the old wooden-handled knives, trying to visualize an arrowhead. "Let's see. I could probably get two arrowheads from each blade." Careful not to nick his knife, Ben pried the wooden handle off. Then with the file, he cut a groove in the blade and broke it in half. Then he filed a point on the piece. Next, he notched the other end.

Ben held up the long, narrow point. "Will it kill a moose?" he wondered, thinking of the big, ungainly animal. "It'll have to do. It's all I've got."

Over the next two days, Ben fashioned twelve arrowheads. His hands were sore and blistered; his wrist hurt from trying to hold the piece steady. But he felt a proud satisfaction in the points. "Not bad for an *ar shu*."

Anxious to test his bow, Ben made several blunt points, saving his arrowheads for big game. To fletch the arrows, he split grouse feathers from the remains of a grouse he had found that was killed by some animal. With a loop of fishing line and pine pitch, Ben attached the feathers to the arrow shaft.

Finally fitting an arrow, Ben tested his bow. It felt like a hunter's bow. His confidence soared. "This might work out after all." He ran his hand over the bow, admiring his work.

The following days, Ben ranged around the camp shooting at dirt clods, rocks, "rabbits" and "grouse" drawn on birch trees with charcoal. At first he felt awkward with the bow, and his shots went wild. But after awhile, Ben began to get the hang of it. He soon discovered, however, that targets stayed still and in plain sight, but game didn't.

After weeks of trial and error, Ben slowly learned to hunt with his bow and arrows. He would take a few steps, then stand and watch, paying attention to sounds and smells around him. Soon he started seeing more game. He found that rabbits would freeze and stay that way until he got too close. Then they would run. The trick was to know exactly how close he could get before the rabbit ran.

One cool morning Ben made his first bow kill.

Moving slowly along a meadow, he saw the grayish brown rabbit standing at the edge of the willows. At first Ben thought it was a smooth brown rock. The animal didn't move. Then it hopped a few steps and froze again. Heart racing, Ben aimed and hit the rabbit in the front shoulders. The rabbit flopped over on its side and kicked a few times, then lay still. Whooping, Ben ran over, grabbed the rabbit, and lifted it up like a trophy.

Ben quickly developed an instinct for when to shoot a rabbit, taking most of them while they sat. But the rabbits were scarce.

Once Ben knew where and how to look for grouse, he begin to take birds as well. The "fool hens," as his Grandfather called them, required little skill to hit. But one species of grouse was trickier. These birds would flush when he got near, making shots difficult. They preferred spruce trees and blended well into the branches.

As Ben honed his hunting skills, he revised his bows. Finding the birch bow too long and awkward to use in the woods, Ben cut off six inches from each end of the bow and reshaped the ends. He discarded the willow bow and replaced it with birch. He modified his bows several times as he gained experience. The hunting bow became a part of Ben.

One evening, Ben sat next to the fire and touched up his arrowheads with the sharpening stone, honing each to a razor's edge. He fitted an arrow and pulled his heavy bow, the arrowhead glittering in the fire light. "It fits right and it feels good." He leaned the bow and quiver against the wall, and gazed at the flames, thinking. *I need something for close up—like a spear. I know just the thing.*

Searching through the cooking gear, Ben pulled out the large butcher knife. "That's got some heavy steel in it." The blade bore the marks of many sharpenings. The dark, discolored handle showed hard use and had a crack in it. One rivet was missing. "The handle ought to come off pretty easy." With the point of his knife, Ben pried the crack open and one side of the handle fell off. Turning the knife over, he worked the other piece off. He held fourteen inches of naked blade in his hand. "I wouldn't want that sticking in me, that's for sure."

Ben sorted through the pieces of birch he'd already cut for the bow, sighted down each one, and chose the straightest piece. With the saw he made a two-inch cut in the end of the shaft. He then fitted the blade into the slot, securing it with a piece of leather boot lace. Then he honed the spear tip to a sharp point.

His work finished, Ben admired his new spear. The twelve-inch blade glittered in the firelight.

# CHAPTER 15

**At the flush of dawn,** Ben crossed the river to check his snares. As he topped out on a rise, he nearly stumbled into a wolf pack. Twenty-five feet below him in a meadow, wolves tore at a moose carcass. Ben counted four adult animals and six pups. "So you're the ones doing all that howling."

Ben's first instinct was to run, but instead he wet a finger and tested the wind. *I'm downwind, so they can't smell me. And there's a lot of meat down there. I'm gonna stick around . . . maybe I'll get a chance to grab some of it.* Ben stepped back into the trees to watch them.

Ears alert, a big, dark-colored wolf turned toward the edge of the clearing. He barked twice, giving an alarm. The others alerted, turning bloody muzzles toward the trees. As Ben turned to look, a grey wolf loped into the clearing. The pack joined in a series of howls. To Ben they appeared hostile, warning the stranger to stay away.

In a challenging walk, ruff up, ears pointed, tail held high, the intruder faced the pack. Then slowly turning, the wolf went into the woods at an easy trot, stopping once to look back. Ben watched him leave.

*You were outnumbered there, but one-on-one would have been a different ball game.*

As soon as the stranger left, the pack resumed feeding on the moose. After what seemed like an eternity to Ben, the wolves began walking away from the kill. After a round of yawning, the pack selected spots in the meadow for naps in the sun. Except for the dark wolf. Ears up, he paced back and forth, sniffing the air, and watching the meadow. Then the wind changed, carrying Ben's scent to the pack. The dark wolf whirled around, facing Ben's direction. Immediately the other wolves leaped to their feet and looked up at the knoll. For a long moment, Ben and the leader stood frozen, staring at each other.

Suddenly, Ben realized he could be in danger. Heart pounding, he stood undecided. He couldn't outrun the wolves; the pack would be on him in a minute. He fitted an arrow in the bow and slowly backed up, his eyes always on the leader. He recalled Grandfather's words, "The Wolf is your totem animal, he will not harm you."

"I hope you're right, Grandpa."

Then, the dark wolf turned and trotted down the valley, followed by other wolves, the pups scampering behind, herded by a black wolf.

Relieved, Ben watched the pack go, leaving a veritable meat market only a basketball shot away! "Grandpa, I hope you're right about wolves leaving the kill." Cautiously, Ben moved down the slope, his senses on high alert. As he neared the moose, he scattered crows and jays. Squawking and scolding, the scavenger birds flew a few feet away, waiting, black eyes riveted on the moose.

Ben inspected the kill. The wolves had eaten the liver, heart and parts of the legs. Bone fragments, loops of white guts, bloody meat droppings, and scraps of hide littered the site. The place smelled of blood and dung. "There's a lot of good meat left." Throwing back his head, Ben whooped with joy. From the ridge, a chorus of howls answered. Startled, Ben laughed. "Thanks, guys."

By this time, Ben had skinned and cleaned several porcupines. Now his experience was paying off. He skinned the moose with relative ease, saving large sections of the hide. One large piece of hide he spread across the ground to put meat on. Starting at a hindquarter, he trimmed the meat off that the wolves had been eating on and tossed the scraps to the scavenger birds. Squawking and pecking, they fought over the pieces. Stretching their wings out to look larger, they ran at each other, defending their territory. Ben sliced along the bone, removing slabs of red meat, marbled with fat. He couldn't believe his good luck.

Ben looked up into the sky. "Someone up there must like me! Man, I can taste the juicy steaks already—medium rare, two inches thick!"

Feeling he wasn't alone, Ben looked up. The lone wolf sat watching him through yellow eyes from some twenty feet away. Startled, Ben stood up, his body tense.

"I don't know you, but you don't seem to be hostile. Maybe Grandfather was right about wolves."

The wolf cocked his head at Ben's voice.

"I think you're after the meat, not me."

The wolf studied Ben.

"Do I pass inspection?" Ben laughed. "Hungry? Guess that's a dumb question, huh wolf? You're eyeballing and sniffing my meat." He picked up a scrap and tossed it toward the animal. On stiff legs the wolf approached watching Ben, snatched the meat and retreated. Ben threw another scrap. Eying him, the animal eased over and grabbed the meat. Gulping the scrap, the wolf faced Ben again.

"Are you trying to be friendly? I could use a little company." The wolf cocked his head and listened like he was trying to understand the strange sounds. "I'm packing this meat to camp, but I'll be back. Stick around."

Ben rolled the hide around the meat and made a bulky pack. The slippery hide was hard to hold, so Ben cut slots for handholds and shouldered the heavy load. It was an awkward carry along with his bow and quiver. He thought about throwing some of the bulky hide away. "No, I might use it for something." On his way to camp, Ben's stomach rumbled at the thought of big, juicy moose steaks. He could hardly wait to try one. But he still had a lot of moose to salvage.

As soon as Ben entered the cave, he spread the meat out on the cool rocks in back, still not able to believe his good luck. He took a piece and smelled it. It gave off a clean, slightly, wild odor. "Man that's gonna be good."

Eager to get back to the kill, Ben picked up his packsack and saw. As he left the cave, the wolf trotted into the clearing. "Well, look who's here. Your buddies run you off ?" Ben asked, happy to see the wolf.

The wolf watched Ben, then looked at the cave opening. "Yeah, that's where I live. I must be pretty ripe if you can smell me from out here." Ben sniffed himself. "I do smell a little gamey."

"You coming?" In a fast stride, Ben crossed the river on the rocks. In a series of effortless leaps, the wolf followed and ranged off to one side. As they neared the kill site, the wolf abruptly stopped and tested the air, then turned toward Ben.

Uneasy, Ben hesitated. "You trying to tell me something, animal?" With a final glance at Ben, the wolf disappeared into the brush. Puzzled, Ben watched him leave. *That wolf knows something I don't. Better take a look.* Careful not to make any noise, Ben topped out on the ridge.

Below him the grizzly ripped at the kill.

Heart pounding, Ben froze. The bitter, metallic taste of fear rose in his throat. He stood downwind of the bear, but when the bear turned his bloody muzzle toward him, Ben's heart stopped. The grizzly reared up to nose the air, powerful muscles rippling under his hide.

Ben faded back into the bush until he was sure the bear couldn't see him, then he raced for the cave. As soon as he was back inside its stone walls, he threw wood on the fire. Ben felt safe around the fire.

*Good thing I paid attention to the wolf. I hate to lose all that good meat, but better he's chewing on the moose than on me.*

# CHAPTER 16

The wolf didn't return that night or the next. After a few weeks Ben gave up on him. Then, early one morning as Ben stepped out of the cave to make his early morning latrine run, the wolf was lying on the flat rock in front of the entrance. Surprised, Ben did a double take.

"You're back. I thought you were gone for good." Ben grinned at the prospect of having the wolf around.

His head cocked, the wolf looked Ben over, giving the rock a couple slaps with his tail. "Well, do I still measure up?" The wolf responded with a tentative wag of his tail.

"I don't have anything to give you. The moose is long gone. No rabbits or grouse around, not even a porcupine. I've been eating fish again. Slim pickings."

The wolf appeared to be losing some fear, but moved back if Ben got too close. He looked Ben up and down again, sniffed at the cave, and then, in an easy run, headed off down the valley. Disappointed, Ben watched him leave. "I could sure use some company. And I'm headed that way too. Need to see what's down there to eat."

Ben loaded the packsack with the saw and axe. Then he tied the moose hide quiver he'd made onto the pack. Ben had made a simple holder by folding a piece of hide over, punching holes along the edge, and sewing it together with fishing line. Ben lifted the pack on and adjusted the straps. He then reached over his left shoulder and pulled out an arrow. He found the position of the quiver awkward and readjusted it until it fit right.

Ben's throat tightened at the thought of going down the valley. When he crossed the river his body alerted, legs tingled. He steeled himself. "Get a hold on it, kid." As he approached the bluffs, Ben saw a cloud of dust rising above the river. Waves of grey and brown forms flowed down the sides of the ridge into the river. The hills moved with life.

Adrenalin surged through him. Ben raced toward the river. Indistinct forms began to take shape. Hundreds of caribou moved down the valley. Clicking of thousands of hooves filled the air. Bleating of the calves trailing the cows, added to the din. Caribou flowed through the valley like a river of horns and hides. Dust and the smell of life hung in the air. By the time Ben got close enough to shoot, the herd had passed, leaving a few stragglers. Shaking with excitement, Ben released an arrow as a caribou climbed out of the river. The shot went high. The animal bolted into the woods. Looking for another target, Ben spotted a caribou dragging its leg. He released an arrow, hitting the animal in the front quarters. Humping, the caribou fled toward a clump of birch trees.

Ben marked the spot in his mind and started to run after caribou, but stumbled to a stop. He remembered Grandfather saying you should wait for an hour before you trail a wounded animal. Gives the animal time to hide and lie down. And once they're down, they'll stiffen up and bleed to death.

Ben looked at his watch. *A whole hour!* He tried not to think of time. He sharpened his arrows to have something to do. Finally Ben couldn't stand it any longer. He looked at this watch. "Only thirty minutes! That should be long enough."

Eagerly, Ben searched the birches without finding any sign of the caribou. "I know I hit that animal. I don't want to lose it." He started a new search higher up on the ridge. About ready to give up, Ben found a spot of blood in the trail. Fitting an arrow, he moved slowly and quietly. He inched along, searching with his eyes. Then he saw the caribou. The animal stood on splayed legs trying to stay up.

The caribou faced Ben, looked him in the eyes. Ben couldn't look away—a living creature watched him, not wanting to die. "I'm sorry." Ben's throat tightened. He maneuvered into position and drew his bow. The eyes followed him. Ben drove an arrow into the caribou's lungs. Taking a few halting steps, the caribou faltered. The front legs collapsed throwing the animal to the ground. The caribou struggled to get up, then fell back, kicked and lay still.

Ben explained to the animal. "I'm sorry. I had to have food. I've got to kill to survive. But I will not waste anything. I promise."

Ben knew there was no other way. Sighing, he took out his knife to clean the caribou, when he heard a bleating. Apprehensive, a calf walked toward him sniffing the air. The animal stopped and watched Ben. Bleating again, the calf moved around him and nuzzled the dead caribou.

"I can't handle this." Waving his arms, Ben shouted, "Get out of here. Get!" Startled, the calf ran into the woods. Ben started cleaning the animal. The calf appeared again at the edge of the woods, watching Ben. "Not again."

Bleating and sniffing the air, the calf looked over at the cow. Frustrated, Ben chased the calf, throwing rocks at it. The animal ran down the valley. Ben watched it leave. Upset, Ben had to get himself together before he could continue. "I'm sorry little guy, I hope you make it."

The wolf loped up and watched Ben's every move. "Hey! What took you so long?" Ben picked up a scrap and tossed it to him. Gulping the meat, the wolf looked up at Ben expectantly. Ben cut another piece and pitched it to the wolf. He finished the meat, sat on his haunches, and gazed at Ben. "That's enough. I've got to pack the rest in."

Ben loaded the hindquarters into the packsack and placed the hide on top. He worked the front quarters up into a tree. "I'll get these tomorrow."

The wolf looked at the meat. "Unless wolves can climb trees, you are outta luck my furry friend. There's lot of good eating in that tree. I don't trust you, animal. I worked too hard for that meat." The wolf sniffed, then stared at Ben, tilting his head as if he didn't understand why. Laughing, Ben said, "I've got you figured out."

Ben made the long hike back, reaching camp in the late twilight, trailed by the wolf. He wedged the hindquarters into a tree near the entrance to cool. The grey wolf stood in the entrance watching Ben. "Sorry, I don't have any scraps. Come around tomorrow." With a final sniff at the tree the wolf loped down the valley.

Ben cooked the heart first. Grandfather said the carcass should cool before cooking, but the heart and liver were O.K. to eat right away. Barely waiting for it to cook through, Ben ate the half-raw meat, wiping his chin with his sleeve.

Ben sat by the fire in a pensive mood. The calf incident had triggered in him a longing for his mother. He could see Mom reading in her favorite chair. She loved to read. Ben smiled. She would be so engrossed in reading, she would sometimes forget she had something on the stove and burn dinner. "Mom," Ben said, getting up to throw wood on the fire. "If I could, I would eat one of your burned dinners in a heartbeat."

Ben awoke early, pulled the hindquarters out of the tree by the entrance and stored them in the back of the cave. Then he hiked back down the valley to bring in the rest of the meat. As he crossed the river, the wolf joined him, still keeping his distance.

"Glad to see you, Boy. Stick with me and I'll give you all the scraps you can eat." Looking in Ben's direction, the wolf turned and headed back into the brush. Disappointed, Ben watched the animal leave. "I was hoping you'd hang around."

As he neared the kill site, Ben stopped and checked the area. He hadn't seen the grizzly since the encounter at the moose kill, but it made him cautious, particularly around a carcass. He listened for birds. Jays squabbled and squawked, but no alarm calls. Ben continued up the ridge. As he broke out of the brush where he'd made the kill, he wasn't alone.

The grizzly!

Across the clearing from Ben, the bear was feeding on the caribou. He had pulled the meat out of the tree. Suddenly, the wind changed and the bear reared up and looked at Ben.

Startled, Ben stumbled and fell, rolling down the hill, dropping his bow and spear. He jumped up and jerked out his knife.

# CHAPTER 17

From out of the bush, the wolf streaked by Ben and charged the grizzly. As the grey closed the gap between them, the grizzly lunged after him. With an easy grace, the wolf jumped clear, chased by the bear. Ben dashed for the closest tree, a dead cottonwood, and hauled himself up into it.

From fifteen feet up in the branches, Ben watched as the wolf harassed the bear, dodging and feinting, evading the grizzly's attack. Pursued by the bear, the wolf disappeared into the thick undergrowth. *He's trying to lead him away!*

Bounding out of the brush, the bear stopped at the gut pile. He held the white gut-loops down with a paw and bit off sections, swallowing the pieces. Stomach contents squeezed out onto the ground. The grizzly licked up the partially-digested food.

Then the bear ambled over to the ribs and started feeding, ripping out chunks of flesh and crushing bones. Awed by the power of those jaws, Ben shivered. The bear fed barely twenty feet from him. Ben reached up for a better grip and snapped a branch. The grizzly erupted into a charge, hitting the cottonwood tree, tearing at the bark with teeth and claws.

The silver tip reared up to his full height and located Ben, its broad head just a few feet below Ben. The grizzly stared into Ben's eyes and he saw death looking at him. In a strained voice, Ben said, "Hootz, I didn't set the trap that tore off your foot or hurt you in any way. I am Ben James of the *Gooch Kaynlye* House."

Wrinkling his lips, the bear exposed yellow teeth set in a bloody muzzle. He studied Ben. He was so close Ben could smell his gut-dung smell. Then he slashed at Ben with six-inch claws, ripping out a chunks of bark. Ben yanked up his feet.

After what seemed like forever to Ben, the grizzly left and went back to the caribou and began feeding again. In terrifying fascination, Ben watched. Massive jaws cracked ribs and ripped off bloody hunks of meat. The bear bit through bones like they were matchsticks. The feeding noises seemed to go on for hours. Ben lost all sense of time.

Finally, the bear stopped and moved back into the brush to a spot overlooking the kill. Realizing he wasn't going to get out of the tree, Ben wedged himself between two limbs. He knew a fall meant death by those crushing and tearing jaws. The long terrifying day finally ended in the hush of the twilight. An even longer, terrifying night followed. Ben thought it would never end. He fought sleep. Nodding, he would jerk awake, fear flooding his body.

Ben dozed off. The nightmare took shape. He was back in Wrangell. Boarded up, the Institute stood dark and deserted. Ben didn't know why he was there. Running back and forth, he tried to get away, but a tall granite fence kept him in. Kids stepped out of the shadows and chased him. They ran alongside and poked sticks at him, crying: "*Ar shur, ar shur*, half-breed, half-breed." They blocked off his only escape, then a big blond kid walked over, grinning. "We got you now, half-breed."

"We got you, half-breed! We got you! We got you! We got you!" the kids chanted. Suddenly, the grizzly charged into the school yard, scattering the screaming kids. Ben tried to run. His legs wouldn't move. Salivating, the grizzly jumped on him, tearing at his body.

Ben jerked awake, disorientated, gasping for breath, heart pounding, afraid of falling.

The long night finally ended. Ben woke up from a fitful, half-sleep and watched the stars fade and the early daylight break. The bear was gone. Ben looked at the edge of the meadow, along the river and in the trees.

Finding no sign of the bear and hearing no alarm calls, Ben debated on what to do. "Well, I'm not going to spend another miserable night in this tree, that's for sure."

Just then, the wolf appeared at the edge of the meadow and ambled over to the cottonwood. Ben could see no alert signs. "I take it you're telling me the bear is gone. Time to haul tail out of here."

Ben scanned the meadow one last time, then climbed down the tree. When he hit the ground his legs collapsed under him. Leaning against tree, he stamped his feet and rubbed his legs until he got circulation going again.

In a wobbling run, Ben snatched the spear and bow and fled the kill site.

After a few minutes of panicked running, Ben slowed to a jog, the wolf by his side. When they reached the cave, the wolf hesitated then followed him in, smelling the meat inside. Bent over, hands on his knees, Ben gulped air. "O.K., Animal, I owe you a meal. You saved my dumb hide again. Just give me a minute. That was a hard run for me."

The wolf barked. "O.K., I got the message." From the meat pile, Ben cut off a slice of caribou and dropped it near the wolf. Without flinching, he took the meat from Ben and left. Ben watched him go. "Sure you won't stick around? Gets pretty lonely."

After the wolf left, Ben sat by the fire reliving the terror of the bear encounter. He had looked into the grizzly's eyes and saw death.

# CHAPTER 18

The following morning, Ben checked the clearing. In the birch tree near the cave, a red squirrel scolded and barked a territorial warning. Down at the river crows squabbled over something. Seeing no movement or sign of the bear, Ben climbed the ridge to the lookout. An early morning haze covered the lower end of the valley.

Ben studied the stream and the meadows as far as he could see. Ducks muttered and a loon fluted from a pond. He shifted his gaze and checked his side of the valley. An eagle rode the air currents above the cliffs, searching for prey, its cry piercing the early morning calm. Ben listened for alarm calls.

In a ragged formation a flock of crows winged by. Ben watched them swooping, diving, and performing roll-overs. "Grandfather said crows go crazy when a bear's around, particularly a grizzly. They don't seemed worried about anything. Looks like they're just having fun."

Relieved, Ben climbed down, his stomach rumbling for more caribou. From the back strap, he cut three steaks and grilled them in the frying pan. Ben ate until he couldn't eat anymore. He had learned to enjoy the moment. The wilderness made the tomorrows uncertain.

Ben set aside some choice steaks for the next few days. Some of the moose meat had gone bad. He wasn't about to lose more meat. He had made a promise to the caribou that no meat would be wasted. And he had remembered a way to keep that promise.

During his fish camp summers, Ben had lived the traditional food gathering life of his people. When he was little, he watched the others prepare and smoke fish. But as he got older his job was to hang pieces of rich, red salmon on the smoking racks. He would smoke the caribou!

From the stand of dead birch, Ben cut poles and dragged them to camp. First, he built two tripods like the ones used in the fish camps, making them as high as he could reach. He placed them in the back of the cave, near the hole in the ceiling. Then he adjusted the distance between the tripods until it looked right, about five feet or so apart. Next Ben lashed horizontal poles on the tripods a foot apart, on both sides, securing them with moose hide thongs.

The rest of the morning, Ben cut the caribou meat into thin strips. It was awkward work for him. He pictured the women at the fish camps laughing and gossiping, filleting salmon with ease in an unbroken rhythm. Ben felt like a clod. But he kept at it, slicing and trimming caribou until late in the day.

When Ben finished he had over two hundred pieces of red meat hanging on the racks. The cow caribou pleading for her life had changed

Ben's view of animals forever. He made sure to use everything he could. He would keep his promise.

The camp robbers and crows soon discovered the scraps. Whenever he threw out a panful, they fluttered around the entrance squabbling and pecking at each other. Somewhat annoyed by the commotion, Ben started to scare them off. Reconsidering, he stopped. "You bird brains are a real pain in the tail. But you might make a good grizzly alarm. And I need all the help I can get."

The next morning, Ben built fires under the rack. The green birch produced a sweet smoke and a natural draft carried it out through the hole in the ceiling. Ben made frequent climbs to the lookout to check for the bear. He worried the grizzly would smell the smoke even though he thought it was probably too high above the valley. Ben couldn't afford to let his guard down. He had seen the power and the killing fury of the bear.

Checking the meat frequently, Ben learned by trial and error how long to smoke caribou. At first the pieces were raw in the center and required more smoking. By late afternoon on the third day, the meat looked and tasted like jerky. As Ben started taking the jerky off the racks, he noticed the meat had lost about half of its weight in the smoking process. "I didn't count on that, but I've still got meat to last for awhile."

Ben's eyes surveyed the cave. He took in the fire pit, smoked meat, smoking racks, stacked firewood, and the spruce-bough bed. The bows, quiver, and spear leaned against the wall next to the bed. *I did it all myself,* he thought with pride. *Maybe I can make it.*

The next morning, Ben fingered the salvaged moose and caribou hides. They needed to be tanned someway. The hides were heavy, covered with a fatty tissue. "This stuff should probably come off."

Tentatively, Ben took his hunting knife and scraped a section off the hide. The tissue rolled up in fatty strips, giving off a musty odor. "Guess that's how it's done." After a day of scraping, his hands were stiff and sore, but the hides looked clean.

He had no idea how to tan a hide, however. "I've read some people used urine. But there's gotta be a better way . . . If smoke will cure meat, maybe it would cure a hide. I'll give it a try." Draping the hides over the smoking rack, Ben built a small fire, adding green birch until he had a thick smoke. Seeing one fire wasn't enough, he built a fire under each hide. A heavy smoke flowed around the hides.

After smoking the hides for a day and a half, Ben decided he'd had enough of wood cutting. He pulled the caribou hide off the rack and examined it. "Pretty stiff. And it smells kinda wild and smokey." Ben wrapped the hide around his shoulders. He could feel the warmth. "Wild and smokey I can live with. Cold I can't."

# CHAPTER 19

Ben dreaded checking the snares. The grizzly was out there somewhere. For reasons he couldn't explain to himself, he always felt safer on his side of the river. As Ben stepped out of the cave, he was surprised to see the wolf lying on a rock near the entrance. Getting up, the animal yawned, jumped off the rock and looked at Ben "Hey! I hoped you'd come back. You saved my tail. Trying to be friendly or you just after my meat? I'm no pushover for a pretty face. Well, maybe Jeannie."

Ben sighed, thinking of the girl in his math class. *What's she doing right now? Does she miss me? What about the other kids from school? What are they doing during their summer vacations? For sure not hunting, smoking caribou, or trying to stay away from a grizzly! Do they know I'm missing yet? Any of them worried about me?*

Sighing again, Ben said, "Jeannie, you're going to have to break some other guy's heart while I'm gone. Right now, I've gotta check some snares. And I'm putting it off. Even the thought of walking the trap line scares the pee out of me."

Ben picked up some meat scraps and tossed them to the wolf. The animal didn't flinch, but ran over and picked them up, then returned to the rock. Watching Ben, the wolf ate the meat.

"Nothing like a free meal, huh wolf?" It was good to talk to someone, even an animal. The wolf cocked his head, looked at Ben and then at the cave. "No, that's all the scraps I've got."

Ears erect, the wolf sat up on his haunches. "Easy Boy, I'm just going down for water." As he walked to the river, the wolf followed him. Hunkered down, Ben cupped his hand and took several drinks. The wolf came over and began lapping water next to him.

"Be my guest." Ben laughed.

"I've gotta check traps. Coming?" Ben started off, glad for the wolf's company. The animal followed, keeping his distance. As Ben crossed the river, his body tingled, his senses tuned to danger. He reached over his shoulder to check the position of the quiver, tightened his grip on his spear and searched the area with his eyes.

The wolf stood nearby watching him, then wagged his tail. "If the bear was around, you wouldn't be wagging." Still cautious, Ben approached the first snare. Empty.

The next held a rabbit caught by the neck. Delighted, Ben couldn't believe his eyes. He had given up on the snares. He grabbed the rabbit by the back legs and clubbed it. "Sorry I had to do that, but I need your body for food." It felt natural to explain to the animal. Ben reset the snare.

The rest of the snares were all empty except for the last one. Caught by one leg, a rabbit struggled to get free. "Wow! Another rabbit." But before Ben could reach it, the wolf snatched the rabbit and began tearing at it. "Hey, that's mine!" Ben yelled as the wolf disappeared into the woods, along with rabbit. "So much for friendship."

That night the wolf entered the cave and watched Ben roast the rabbit. "That's a surprise. What's going on in that wolf mind of yours? Thought I'd seen the last of you for today." The wolf sniffed the cooking smells and looked toward the rabbit. "Forget it, animal. You got all the rabbit you're going to get for today" The wolf looked at Ben and gave a tentative wag of his tail.

"O.K., O.K." Ben said, tossing out a handful of jerky from the rack, "I'm an easy touch." The wolf carried the jerky to a spot near the entrance and ate the meat. Then, with a couple thumps of his tail, he ambled out into the night. Ben ran outside hoping he'd be laying on his rock. But the wolf was gone. "I thought you'd stay this time." Disappointed, Ben returned to the cave.

The next morning Ben awoke with a start, feeling something wet touch his face. Startled, he looked up at a grey face and yellow eyes staring down at him.

"What did you do, give me a lick?"

Slowly, Ben sat up, delighted that the wolf seemed to be accepting him. Making a low ow owww sound in his throat, the wolf wagged his tail. He was still wary though. Any sudden movement from Ben startled him.

Not wanting to scare the wolf off, Ben eased up slowly and went outside for a pee. Circling the clearing, tail straight out, the wolf also marked his territory. "Does that mean you're gonna stay?"

"If you're gonna stay, I should give you a name. How about White Fang?" Tilting his head, the wolf listened. "No, you're not a White Fang. How about King, the famous Yukon Husky?" Ears alert, the wolf stared at Ben. "Nope. That's not right either. Well then, how about Wolf? Just plain Wolf." The wolf wagged his tail. "Wolf it is then."

Wolf rubbed up against Ben, sending a thrill through him. Ben reached down and gave the animal a tentative pat on the neck. Lifting his head, Wolf burst into a full howl, ending in a long drawn-out cry. Caught up in the moment, Ben tried a howl. Throwing back his head, he throated a high-pitched, cowboy yell. Instantly, Wolf joined in, undulating at a slighter lower pitch, his eyes sparkling, changing to hues of green and amber. Something Ben could not explain passed between them—he knew Wolf had accepted him.

After a shared meal of dried caribou, Wolf made a place by the fire, digging it out and trying it for comfort several times until he was satisfied. Then he flopped down. Ben laughed at Wolf's bed making. "Warmest spot in the whole place and you've taken it over. Thanks a lot."

Ben watched the flames, thinking of Mom. She loved sitting around a campfire and arguing with the men. She had an opinion on everything . . . and a solution.

Ben smiled recalling her and the boxing lessons. He was in the eighth grade, his last year at the Institute. On the way home from school, Victor and Charlie Tagish jumped him. No reason. Just pure meanness. When he walked in the door, Mom surveyed his torn shirt and bruises. "That half-breed business again?"

Ben nodded.

Pursing her lips as she always did when she was angry, Mom said, "If you've got to fight, you might as well do it right." She arranged for him to take boxing lessons from Frank Javier, a former professional boxer from the Philippines.

The lessons came in handy. The fall after graduation they moved to Seattle. Ben looked forward to his freshman year: a new school, a new start. But his first day at Hill Crest High School, the Indian thing came up again. The details were still sharp in his mind.

He was on his way to class when he saw the bully trailed by two tagalongs. Ben recognized the type. He'd met them in Wrangell. White or Indian they were all the same. The big blond kid stepped in front of him.

"Where you going Tonto?" Blondie sneered. "I'm selling insurance. Might call it health insurance." He laughed at his own wit. "Let's have your lunch money. I'll be around to collect every day. You pay, you stay healthy." Thrusting his face into Ben's, he snarled, "Get it, Tonto? Understand, Kimo Sabe?"

"Yeah, I understand."

"I thought you would."

Blondie turned to his cronies. "See, no sweat."

"Do you understand this?" Ben said in a hard voice. He assumed the boxer's stance: shoulder turned to the bully, head down, feet apart, left hand curled loosely just below his left eye to protect his chin, right hand held to the right of his chin, elbows close to the body.

"Hey everyone, Geronimo wants to fight!" A crowd materialized around them.

"Try this for size, Redskin," the blond kid yelled as his shoulder dropped, signaling a punch was coming. Ben dodged the blow, then moved in and hit him with two right hand jabs to the face.

"Damn Indian!" the kid screamed, blood pouring down his face from his nose and smashed lip. He charged Ben, throwing wild punches. Weaving and bobbing, Ben blocked and dodged the blows. Then he stepped in and hit Blondie again with two left jabs.

Trying to evade the blows, the bully stumbled and fell. Ben put his foot on the kid's chest, holding him down. "Hey, White Eyes," Ben said, loud enough for the gathered crowd to hear, "When you call me a damn Indian, you'd better smile." It was a line he remembered from a movie. Then he turned, his blood up, ready to take on the other two on, but they had disappeared around the corner of the gym.

The crowd cheered and applauded.

"By the way, Blondie," Ben said to the kid still sprawled on the ground.

"I just cancelled that health insurance policy."

Just then a pretty girl with a brown ponytail walked by and flashed him a smile. Ben smiled back. "It must be my Indian blood," he said, loud enough for her to hear. That became quite a popular saying around school.

Later Ben would meet the pony-tailed girl in his math class: Jeannie. Laughing to himself, Ben got up and tossed a log on the fire. "Must be my Indian Blood."

# CHAPTER 20

**Ben studied his "calendar."** When he first settled in the cave, he had been pretty careful to make a mark on the wall each morning with charcoal. But after a while it didn't seem to matter anymore. Sometimes he forgot; sometimes he just didn't bother. As far as Ben could tell, it was about the middle of August.

The old people called August, *Sa ha sa*, the Moon of the Ripe Berries. The name perfectly described the valley. It had erupted with berries, ripening in orbs of red, black, yellow, and orange fruit. Whenever Ben found a berry patch, he gorged himself on blackberries, strawberries, raspberries, huckleberries, high bush cranberries, and berries he couldn't identify.

Ben always approached berry patches with caution, watching Wolf, listening to bird calls, and scouting the perimeters. He often found bear tracks and tar-colored droppings among the fruit-heavy bushes. He was relieved when he didn't find the mangled track of the grizzly. The smaller tracks were obviously made by black bears, but Ben never let his guard down. "Wolf, we haven't come across grizzly tracks for over a month. You think maybe he's left the country?" Wolf looked up, moving his head like he was trying to understand the sounds. Giving Wolf a pat, Ben worked the idea over in his mind: *Probably not.*

On his side of the river, Ben found patches of wild roses growing along the bank. He recognized the plant because he had helped his mother pick them. She made jelly and from the fruit she called rose hips. And Grandfather dried the hips and made tea. The hips contained vitamin E. Or was it C? He couldn't remember.

Ben examined one of the fruits. "Not ripe yet. Mom always picked these after the first frost, sometime in September or October."

Yearning for potatoes or rice to go with the meat, Ben tried to remember what Grandfather had said about water lily roots and how the Indian people gathered them for food. "I'll have to give those ponds a looking over."

With Wolf running ahead looking for rodents, Ben hiked to a pond that was next to the river. Moose tracks indented the muddy shore. "Wolf, here are the plants Grandpa talked about. Wish I'd paid more attention. I don't know if these things are ripe or not."

"Well, there's only one way to find out." Laying his bow and spear on the bank, Ben took off his shoes and Levis and waded out into the pond, sinking nearly to his knees in the mud. He broke off a water lily and shook it. Black seeds rolled off. He picked several seeds and tasted them. "I don't know about these. Maybe they need to be dried. But the moose seem to like 'em. What do you think, Wolf?"

Curious as to what Ben was doing, Wolf came over and sniffed the water lily. Puzzled, he tilted his head and stared at Ben, then yawned and flopped down in the sun. "It must be nice to sleep in the sun while I'm freezing my buns off." Wolf gave a few half-hearted wags of his tail and went to sleep.

Harvesting the roots and seeds of the lilies proved to be a cold, muddy job. With a long stick, Ben dug lilies out, holding the plants by the head so as not to lose any ripe seeds. While digging lilies, Ben found another plant with a large root stock. It was a silver colored, feathery-leaved plant growing along the shore.

"This is another plant Grandpa showed me. But I don't remember what he said." He peeled one of the roots and took a tentative bite. "Tastes kinda like a carrot. I could use them for roasts and stews." In a week of cold, wet, muddy work, Ben gathered a packsack full of roots and seed pods.

A few days later, in digging out a rodent, Wolf uncovered the root of a grassy plant. Curious, Ben picked up the white bulb and sniffed it. It had a strong, sharp smell. He took a tentative bite. "An onion! And a strong one too! You did good, Wolf." Ben held the onion under Wolf's snout. Wrinkling his nose, Wolf stared up at Ben, who laughed. "Not on your list of edibles, huh?" The plant grew in abundance in the sandy soil. Ben gathered all he could find.

As they returned to camp, Wolf stopped at the edge of a blueberry patch, sniffing the air. "What is it?" Wagging his tail, Wolf looked up at Ben. "You don't look too worried. Are you trying to tell me you found something else to eat?" Ben wetted a finger and tested the wind. Whatever it was couldn't scent him. "Let's check it out." Fitting an arrow, Ben cautiously approached the patch.

Fifty feet away, the bushes shook and jerked as a dark shape stripped berries. A black bear reared up sniffing the wind. Ben wasn't sure, but he thought black bears were edible. He quietly fitted an arrow and drew his bow. Then he heard Grandfather's voice in his head, "Take only what you need."

Wolf waited, shivering with excitement. Ben lowered his bow. "We don't need any more meat right now, Wolf. Let him go." Wolf looked up at Ben, then at the bear and then back at Ben. Suddenly, the wind shifted and the bear caught their scent. With a "Woof" it streaked down the valley. Wolf stared at the bear until it was out of sight.

"I take it you don't agree," Ben said, bending over to scratch Wolf under his chin, a favorite spot. Wiggling in ecstasy, Wolf lifted his muzzle for more. "Hope I'm forgiven."

Back in the cave, Ben experimented with the roots he had dug up. He let the fire die down to a bed of hot coals, then piled the embers over two large roots to bake. While they cooked, he put water in the frying pan and added jerky, onions, water lily seeds, roots, and the wild "carrots." He put the stew over the coals to cook. When the roots were soft to the point of his knife, Ben raked them out. Peeling the skin off one, he salted and peppered it and took a tentative bite. "Not bad. Tastes a little bit like a potato." He gave Wolf a piece of the "potato." Wolf smelled it and gave it a lick, but wouldn't eat it.

"Not your favorite, huh?"

When the stew bubbled and began giving off caribou odors, Wolf perked up. "I thought that might get your attention." With a tin cup, Ben scooped out a plate of stew. Wolf ran over, sniffing. "I don't think cooked stuff is good for you." He gave Wolf a handful of jerky instead. "Now it's my turn for a little chow," he said, tasting a bite of the stew. "Hey! That's really good. Just needs a little more salt."

Ben sat next to the fire thinking of food. "Roots and seeds are going to work out O.K. I should've paid more attention to Grandpa. Probably more edible stuff out there. I sure wish we hadn't lost the front quarters of that caribou. We're going through jerky fast."

# CHAPTER 21

After the first frost, Ben returned to the rose patch, now heavy with bright red fruit. He filled the coffee pot many times, dumping the hips into the packsack. When Ben got tired of picking, he returned to the cave and spread the fruit out on flat rocks next to the fire. When he ran out of space there, he spread fruit on the natural shelf above it to dry. The shelf proved to be an ideal place. The heat and smoke dried the fruit in two days. Ben picked rose hips for a week. After drying the hips, he had nearly a packsack full. "That's it for a while. I've got to do some hunting."

That night Ben sat by the fire and sipped rose hip tea. He found that three rose hips made the best tea. Ben threw wood on the fire and crawled into bed, but lay awake worrying about food. *Winter's coming and I'm about out of jerky. Snares aren't catching anything anymore. Don't know what happened to the rabbits. And I haven't seen a moose track for weeks.* Ben pulled the caribou hide over him and fell into a troubled sleep.

The caribou cow appeared to Ben in his dream. She stood in a grassy meadow at the edge of a stand of white birch. The cow looked at him with kindness in her eyes. The scene faded and he found himself back at the first camp where the plane had crashed. Grandfather was bathing in the lake. When Ben walked up, Grandfather smiled at him from a face unmarked by age or pain. Looking at Ben, he said, "Grandson, this is the way of the *Kolosh.*" Then he was gone.

Ben woke up in the darkness, puzzled by the dream. Then it came to him: the caribou was forgiving him for killing her because he had kept his promise not to waste anything. And Grandpa was telling him to perform the ancient purification ritual. It was worth a try.

Ben began at daylight. He remembered Grandfather saying that *Dikaankaawu* required a hunter to fast and bathe before hunting big game. He had never fasted before and didn't know exactly what was expected, other than going without food. But he knew it was a religious thing, so he did no work except to keep the fire going. Otherwise he rested.

The next morning, Ben went down to the river carrying soap and a towel. Along the bank he found a place where the water formed a backwater pool. Ben undressed and waded into river. The shock of the cold water took his breath away. His legs tingled with pain and his testicles felt like they had been tightened in a vise. When he finally caught his breath, Ben soaped his body and hair, then plunged under the water to rinse. Gasping, Ben climbed out on the bank, his body shivered, still recoiling from the shock. Ben grabbed the towel with shaking hands, dried off and got dressed.

When his body returned to a normal temperature, Ben stretched out his arm and faced the morning sun. "*Dikaankaawu*, I have fasted and purified myself. Hear my prayer. I come before you to ask for your help. I need food for the winter and blankets for my bed. I cannot survive without these things. I am going into your woods to hunt. Please send one of your animals to me. I will not waste anything."

His prayer complete, Ben crossed the river and walked along the trail to the ponds, hunting for moose. Wolf ranged slightly ahead, as he normally did. Ben scouted the ponds without finding a single track. He then tried the lower valley, hoping to jump a caribou. Finally, he gave up. Wolf tested the air several times and looked at Ben. "Yeah I know. There's nothing out there." Disappointed Ben returned to the cave.

"Maybe *Dikaankaawu* didn't hear my prayer. I really felt good about fasting and bathing, but I guess it didn't work out. Oh well, we've still got a lot of daylight left. Let's pick some rose hips before they get too ripe."

As they neared the rose patch, a moose stepped out of the willows scarcely twenty feet from them, catching Ben and Wolf by surprise. The young bull turned and looked in their direction. Reacting, Ben eased an arrow out of the quiver. Slowly drawing back the bow, he released the arrow, hitting the bull in the lungs. The animal hunched up and walked toward them. Ben drove another arrow into the bull's chest. Wolf leaped at the bull, grabbing him by the throat. Ben ran up and put an arrow into the moose's heart, burying the shaft to the feathers. The bull fell over, struggled to get up, then sank back down and lay still.

Ben couldn't believe what had just happened. He replayed the scene in his mind. "That moose walked right to us. Never ran, never showed fear. Did you see that, Wolf? You were right Grandpa, that was no coincidence. *Dikaankaawu* answered my prayer. He sent the moose."

Ben sat on a rock next to the dead moose. "I'm sorry you had to die, but I promise you I will not waste anything. To waste is not he way of the *Kolosh*."

# CHAPTER 22

With Wolf in the lead, Ben made his morning climb to the lookout to check for the grizzly and look the country over. "Wolf, the only thing I see out there is cold weather and we gotta get ready for it."

As they came off the lookout, Ben eyed the cave entrance, speculating on how to close it in. The trunks of two birch trees closed one end of the dome-shaped opening. "I can run a short wall behind the trees and make the door there. Let's get with it, Wolf. Thinking about it won't keep us warm."

With his eye, Ben measured from the second birch tree and marked out a door, then stepped through the door opening. "It's a little bit wide." Erasing the line with his foot, he scratched another line. "That looks about right. So, that leaves me with about two feet of wall behind the birches and another two feet or so for the main wall to build. But with what?"

Ben's eyes zeroed in on the rocks littering the ground along the edge of the cliffs. "Got plenty of rocks. That might be just the thing." With a flat rock he cleaned out the debris in front of the cave. Wolf came over, sniffed ground and looked up at Ben. "Nothing to do with eating. Now move out of my way." Gently, he pushed Wolf aside.

Ben started laying rocks behind the birches. He selected the flattest pieces for the bottom row. By late day, he had the walls up. "Door height is a little low for me. I'll have to remember to duck so I don't hit my head." Ben stepped back and looked at his job, nodding in approval. "Looks pretty nifty, Wolf. Gotta fill the gaps someway."

The next day, Ben went down to the river and made a mud puddle, adding leaves and pine needles. When Wolf started to wander off, Ben called him back and scratched him around the ears. "Stay with me, Wolf. I'm mixing some mud and need you close in case the grizzly tries to jump me." He filled the frying pan with mud and began plastering the gaps in the wall.

At first he tried using a flattened stick, but his hands worked out better. It was cold, muddy work and he had to stop several times to warm up by the fire. Ben plastered both sides of the wall, touching up spots he missed.

"Wolf, I think we'll call that good for today. Not a bad job, if I say so myself."

The next morning, Ben looked at the opening, trying to come up with a way to attach a door. "I could make a door out of logs, but what would hold them together?" He fingered the moose hide. "I could tie them together with rawhide straps."

"Come on, Wolf." From the slide-killed trees, Ben selected the straightest lodgepole pines, all about four inches in diameter. He cut down the trees, limbed them, and dragged the trunks to the cave. Ben tried to visualize how he would hold the door in place. "I've got it! I'll build the door to slide across the opening from the inside of the cave."

Ben stood a pole up against the opening and marked the length with a piece of charcoal. He sawed the pole to length and tried the fit at the highest point of the mouth, then he cut the rest of the poles to the same length. Ben laid out the poles side by on the floor. From the salvaged moose hide, he cut long straps, tied the poles together. It made for an all day job. At the final tie, Ben was eager to see how the door worked.

Ben started to lift it in place, but it was heavier than it looked. He strained to get it into position. "It fits! A few gaps between the logs—I'll fill those with mud. But I think it's gonna work." He tried sliding it open and shut. It took some serious muscle to operate. It had been a busy three days, but Ben knew he had to get ready for winter. He'd probably be in the cave at least until freeze-up, maybe longer.

The next day, Ben looked at the meat shelf. "Wolf I see by the scratches that someone tried to get into the meat cache. You wouldn't know any-thing about that, would you?" Wolf looked up and gave the floor a slap with his tail.

"You couldn't quite reach the jerky, but a bear could clean us out." Ben's eyes searched the cave for a solution. He noticed a ledge near the highest part of the roof. "Meat would be safe up there. But I'll need some kind of a ladder."

From straight lodgepole pines, Ben constructed a ladder, tying it together with raw hide straps. Late in the day, he lifted the ladder into place.

"Wolf, let's give it a whirl." Ben took a tentative step onto the first crosspiece.

"Looks like it's gonna hold." He climbed up the ladder and inspected the shelf. "Perfect. No animal can reach it. Well, mice might. I'd better take down the ladder when I'm not using it. What a pain." Ben loaded the jerky into the packsack and carried it up to the cache. Wolf watched him work.

That night lying on his spruce bed, wrapped in the caribou hide, Ben surveyed the cave: the new wall, the door, the food cache, the ladder. "Not too shabby, Ben. Not too shabby."

# CHAPTER 23

**Ben stood at the entrance** of the cave watching Vs of geese and ducks fly over, the thrust of wings, honks, yelps, and quacks filled the morning sky. Wistfully, he watched them. "They're going south, Wolf. I wish we could go with them." For a moment scenes of home flooded Ben's memory.

Ben shook off the past. He shivered thinking of the coming winter. He no longer thought of rescue, only survival.

He made a decision. "Wolf, we haven't seen a sign of the grizzly since the caribou kill. If we're gonna be stuck here, I want to know what's out there. What kind of country this valley empties into. That's our way out."

Ben slipped on the pack and picked up his heavy hunting bow and his quiver of arrows. Wolf knew the signs. Bright eyed, ears erect, he "talked" to Ben with whines and short woofs. "I take it you're ready to go exploring. O.K. Let's head out." Ben pointed down the valley. Wolf took the lead, frequently stopping to smell the air.

Nearing the caribou kill site, Ben tensed. Fitting an arrow, he checked the clearing for fresh grizzly sign. A crow pecked at something in the sand. Little was left of the caribou except for bone fragments. The top of the caribou's skull had been bitten off to get at the brains. The cottonwood bore marks of the bear's fury. Sections of bark had been torn out by tooth and claw. Ben's throat tightened, the attack still vivid in his mind.

Wolf came racing back. "Let's get out our tails out of here. This place gives me the creeps. Just stay close." Relieved to have Wolf next to him, Ben continued down the game trail. "Wolf, I don't want any surprises. You're my eyes, ears, and nose in grizzly country," Ben said, stroking Wolf. "Stay close." As he turned a bend in the river, Ben couldn't believe his eyes. A log structure showed through the trees. "Look! Wolf! Look!" He shouted, pointing at the building. "A cabin! A cabin!" Racing forward. Ben shouted, "Hello! Hello!" Wolf, thinking it was a game, dashed ahead.

Breaking stride, Ben stopped, disappointed by what he saw. The lean-to cabin sat at the edge of a stand of lodgepole pine. Gaps showed between the logs. The hewn log door hung open on rawhide-strap hinges, creaking in the wind. Brown, frost-killed weeds covered the dirt roof. Waist high weeds and saplings reclaimed the area, a cold wind rattled dead stalks and scattering leaves along the ground.

Wolf rubbed against Ben. "It's O.K. I was just expecting too much. No one's been here for years." Disappointed, Ben opened the door and stepped into the dark, windowless cabin. An air of decay and wood smoke hung in the place.

To his right, a shaft of light came through a hole in the roof. As his eyes adjusted, he could see a table against the opposite wall. Directly in front of him a bunk stretched across the back wall. Wolf brushed by Ben and ran over to the bunk. He barked once and looked back at Ben. "You think we could use a few blankets, Wolf?" Ben went to the bed.

A skull grinned up at him from a sleeping bag.

On rubbery legs, Ben bolted through the door, falling over Wolf. Scrambling up, Ben grabbed a tree for support, gasping for air, the bile rising in his throat. He thought he was going to lose his breakfast. Wolf rubbed up against him, making low throaty sounds.

Ben caught his breath, "I'm O.K. Guess a dead man can't hurt us. Come on, Wolf. Let's try it again." Still queasy, Ben forced himself to return to the bunk and its grisly occupant. Pieces of mummified skin topped with matted black hair clung to the skull. The skeleton lay in a partially open sleeping bag, one bony arm hung over the side, encased by the remnants of a jacket sleeve. Directly below the skeletal hand, Ben spotted an open notebook. He picked it up and noticed something scrawled across a page. Ben held it up to the light and puzzled out the writing.

*bear jumped me*

*not going to make it*

*goodbye*

"A bear killed him, Wolf." For a minute, he relived his own terror in the cottonwood tree. "That could've been me," he whispered, staring at the skeleton, uncertain about what to do. "Like it or not, Wolf, I've got to bury him. It's not right for him to go unburied."

Ben found a shovel leaning against the wall and started for the door. "Come on, Wolf." On a sandy bench at the side of the cabin, he selected a spot overlooking the river and outlined a grave, two feet by six feet. The soil was easy to dig except for the tree roots. At three feet, he hit rock. "I think that's it."

Ben steeled himself for the next part—moving the skeleton. He hesitated at the door, "I've gotta do it." He took a deep breath and entered the cabin. Trying not to look at the skull, which watched him through empty sockets, Ben pulled the sleeping bag up and over the skull. But the hardest part was yet to come—the arm! His throat tight, Ben forced himself to lift the skeleton's arm by the jacket sleeve and eased it into the sleeping bag.

Ben dragged the sleeping bag onto the floor and out to the grave site, as gently as possible. Then he positioned the sleeping bag alongside the grave and lowered it into the hole. Halfway down, the arm slipped back out of the bag. Ben shook his head, "I'm not putting your arm back in again. Sorry. It was hard enough the first time."

Ben quickly began shoveling dirt over the skeleton. The first shovelfuls made a rattling noise when they hit the sleeping bag. An eerie, unnerving sound. With the edge of the shovel, Ben raked in dirt. The rattling stopped, replaced by the familiar thud of dirt on dirt. Finishing, Ben stood at the grave, not sure of what he should do or say. "If I make it out of here, I'll tell the authorities about you. Your family would want to know."

# CHAPTER 24

**With the dead man** buried, Ben felt better about examining the cabin. He went over to check the log table, set with a tin plate, cup, knife, fork, and mice-tattered shreds of a salt bag. A candle stuck in a bottle had provided light. Another bottle sat on a shelf above the table. Uncorking it, Ben sniffed the contents. "Smells like booze, Wolf." Piled on the shelf were mineral specimens together with mouse-chewed candles and matches. Ben examined a heavy rock, streaks of a dark mineral running through it. "Looks like he was a prospector."

Then Ben noticed a pack frame and packsack hung from the ceiling by a rawhide thong. He cut it down and carried it over to the table. Eagerly Ben searched the pack. On the top lay a bundle of rawhide straps. "Probably left from his furniture making. Just what I need." Next, he pulled out a sack. Inside he found white beans. Delighted, Ben scooped out a handful and let the beans trickle through his fingers. "Wow! Beans! Man, can I use these." Then, a tin box of tea. Ben read the label: "Red Rose. Fine Teas Since 1890." He opened the can and smelled the spicy fragrance of black tea. In the bottom of the pack was a partial sack of flour, a box of salt, a pair of socks and three candles.

"Look at all this food and stuff, Wolf. Beans to go along with the jerky. Man oh man! What a treat. Tea! I can't believe our luck. This is like Christmas." He repacked the food and leaned the pack against the wall.

Then Ben checked the fire pit on the opposite wall. Wood had been stacked neatly along the wall. In the ashes of a long-dead fire, a frying pan set next to a coffee pot. Ben examined the pan. "Some kind of food, worked over by the mice." Wolf had to smell it. "Satisfied?" Next, Ben inspected coffee pot. "Looks like tea. Probably his last meal." Ben stopped, saddened by the prospector's death. "I'm sorry, Guy."

Ben soon shook off the feeling and continued his inventory. Next to the fire pit, an axe leaned against the wall, along with a gold pan and prospector's pick. Attached to a rawhide strap, a slab of something covered with green mold hung from the ceiling. Ben inspected it. "Looks like bacon. Don't think I wanna eat that." Wolf sniffed at the slab. "No, you don't," Ben warned, pushing Wolf's nose aside. "And don't give me that look."

Interested in the construction details, Ben checked the bunk, which was made of peeled birch poles that stretched across the back wall. "I see you used notches and rawhide thongs to fasten the parts together. Kinda like Lincoln logs. You were pretty handy with the axe."

Then Ben saw it. A rifle! It lay along the inside edge of the bunk rail. Excited, he grabbed the rifle. "Look at this, Wolf! A gun, a gun! What a find!" Ben shouldered the rifle and sighted down the barrel. Working the lever, he ejected an empty cartridge case. He levered the action again, but the rifle was empty. "There's gotta be ammo here someplace."

Ben ran his hand over the blued metal and the walnut stock. The sling gave off a faint leathery-oil odor. At the door, he read the stamping on the side of the barrel: 348 Winchester. "A little rusty, but overall it's in good shape." Slinging the rifle on his back, he stalked around the room. Ben liked the feel of the Winchester.

"Wolf, let's find some ammo for this gun." Ben searched the bunk, feeling along the edge for cartridges. He checked around the table and along the walls. Frustrated, Ben dumped the pack out onto the table and searched through the contents again, then checked all the pockets. "What did you do with your ammo?" Ben snapped. Recognizing the tone, Wolf whined and rubbed against his legs. "I'm O.K. Just teed off. It doesn't make sense. There's gotta be some shells here somewhere. Not too many places to hide things." Ben sighed. There was no where else to look. "Even if I can't find ammo, it's a neat rifle. I'm keeping it."

At the head of the bunk, a belt knife hung from a peg. Ben slipped the knife out of the sheath and looked it over. The six-inch blade showed a slight rust, but was razor sharp. On the side of the sheath, a pocket held a sharpening stone. "Great, we could use another knife."

"Well, that about does it." Ben gave the place a final look over to see if he had missed anything. Then he remembered something had dropped when he was hauling out the body. Curious, but wary it might be some part of the skeleton, Ben peered under the bed. Once his eyes adjusted to the darkness, he saw a shiny object on lying on the floor. He grabbed it and brought it to the light, hoping it was a cartridge. "A dead man's watch. Creepy."

Ben opened the cover and read the flowery script etched inside:

*To John*

*Together for ever*

*Your loving wife*

*Laura*

"So that's your name: John! Well, John that's a pretty nifty watch. I'll try to find Laura and give it back to her." Ben stuck it in his pocket. "Let's see what we can use." He made a pile on the table of everything he wanted to salvage: the Winchester, packsack, axe, frying pan, coffee pot, candles, sheath knife, gold pan, pick, and shovel.

Ben built a fire and pulled up the chair to sit in. "Beats sitting on a rock." Getting up, he examined the chair. "John, you were a good man with an axe and rawhide." Ben lifted it. "Not too heavy. I could carry this. It'd be neat to have by the fire. I'm going to take it with me."

Wolf barked to go out. "No, I want you here tonight. This place is too spooky." The image of the bed and its skeletal occupant haunted Ben. He put more wood on the fire, leaned up against the wall next to the warmth, and fell into a half-sleep.

The next morning, Ben looked through the cabin one last time to see if he'd missed anything. In a corner, he found the cleaning rod and gun oil. Ben lashed the chair to the pack with a piece of rawhide. He slipped on the pack, picked up the rifle and bow. "That's it, Wolf. Let's go home." But before they walked through the doorway, Ben hesitated. He went back inside, grabbed the bottle of whiskey and stuck it in the pack.

"You never know. We might need this for something."

# CHAPTER 25

As Ben hiked back to the cave, the valley lay quiet, still shadowed by the morning sun. Frost edged the river. Ben listened to the familiar feeding sounds of water fowl. The trail skirted a beaver pond and as they passed, a beaver slapped the water with its tail. Startled, Ben's heart raced. Finding the prospector's skeleton had Ben on full alert.

Ben watched Wolf sniffing the breeze. "Anything out there, Wolf?" Wolf turned and gazed lazily at Ben. "Guess not. I hope it stays that way." Ben scanned the trail ahead. As he patted Wolf Ben noticed Wolf's fur was getting thicker. "I'm going to have to do something about winter duds myself. Grandpa's jacket isn't going to be warm enough."

Ben and Wolf returned to a cold cave.

As he set about building a fire, Ben worked over in his mind the idea making some kind of winter clothing.

Taking the caribou hide from his bed, Ben visualized a coat. He had been using the skin for a blanket. Ben made several sketches on the cave floor before settling on a poncho-like garment. With the hide spread out flesh up, he scratched out the cuts with a stick and marked them with a piece of charcoal. Cutting along the lines, he ended up with a rectangle.

With line from Grandfather's reel, Ben started sewing the two sides together, hair side out. It was punch two holes with the awl blade, push the needle through the holes, make a loop, pull the stitch tight... then do it again and again, over and over. Slow tedious work. But Ben had learned patience. Sitting by the fire in John's chair, he worked on the coat all day and into the evening, leaving openings for his arms and head.

When Ben tied off the last stitch, he gave a sigh of relief. Eagerly, he slipped the poncho on. The hide was stiff, but warm. He liked the light brown color. Ben grinned. "Not too bad," he told himself. "Not too bad." That night Ben wore his new poncho to bed.

The next day Ben made sleeves from the salvaged moose hide. He planned to roll the hide into tubes and sew the "sleeves" onto the poncho, but the stiff hide wouldn't roll up. The best shape he could make was a rough oval shape. He sewed the edges of the "ovals" together, then attached the sleeves to the coat.

Ben modeled his coat for Wolf, who came over and nosed it. "Does it meet with your sniff test?" Ben teased. "I think it's pretty neat, Wolf." Looking up, Wolf wagged his tail. "Well, I think it's better than a one-tail-wag-coat. *I made it*. Wasn't born with a fur coat like you-know-who." With the shaving mirror, Ben looked at himself from different angles to see his handiwork.

Flush with his success, Ben started right to work on a pair of moose-hide mittens. The cutting and sewing went faster this time. He had the technique worked out and made tight, even stitches. The mitten was simply a wide oval sewn shut at one end with a smaller oval added for the thumb. After another day of sewing, Ben tied off the last stitch. Anxious to try them, he slipped his hands into the mittens. Immediately, he felt the warmth. "Man, that feels so good! Pretty stiff though. Maybe they'll soften up. Overall, not too shabby."

Sticking a mitten under Wolf's nose, Ben asked, "What do you think?" Sniffing, Wolf eyed Ben. "Yeah, it's no big deal for you. But you could show a little appreciation for my skill. Freeze my hands and I can't cut wood to keep you warm while you laze by the fire." Ben said, laughing at Wolf's puzzled expression. Wolf gave him two tail wags this time.

Next, Ben started work on head gear. He wrapped a piece of hide around his face and head to get the size. Then he sewed up the side and top. Pulling the cap over his head, Ben marked the mouth and eye positions with charcoal, then cut them out. The hat looked like a furry ski mask with a crest on top. When Ben tried it on, Wolf backed away-stiff legged, ruff up. "Did I scare you, Boy?" Ben said, taking off the cap so Wolf could smell it. "See, it's me under there."

It was late and Ben had been working several long days. He banked the fire and crawled into bed wearing the coat, then pulled the moose skin over him. *Things are looking up. Now I'm set for winter clothes. Got a blanket for my bed. And I've got a couple hundred pounds of moose jerky in the cache.*

*Think I'm going to make it!*

Wolf curled up next to him. From out of the night came the howl of the pack. Jumping up, Wolf ran to the door, woofing once. "O.K. O.K. Hold your horses." Prying himself out of a warm bed, Ben shoved the door aside so Wolf could squeeze through. A cold blast of air hit him. Shivering, Ben crawled back in bed. "I've got to give some serious thought to Telegraph Creek," he told himself.

# CHAPTER
# 26

During the night, Ben felt Wolf curl up next to him again. He reached over and gave Wolf a pat, then went back to sleep. He was used to Wolf's frequent nighttime absences, but he always felt relieved when Wolf returned.

The next morning, Ben got up and pushed the door closed. "That really helps to keep this place warm. There must be a foot of snow out there." Shivering, he built up the fire and put water on for tea and jerky broth. Warming his hands, Ben looked over at Wolf still curled up by the bed. "Hey! Get your furry tail outta the sack. You gonna sleep all day?"

With a stretch and a yawn, Wolf got up and followed Ben outside into a white wilderness for their morning latrine run. Wolf tested the morning breeze. Ears alert, he looked once at Ben, then raced around the clearing, leaping and nipping at the snow. "Wolf, don't eat any yellow snow," Ben joked.

"I'm glad somebody's happy in this stuff. But I don't have big furry feet like you do to get around in the snow. Well, big maybe, but not furry," Ben laughed as he buttoned up his Levis. "Come on, Wolf. It's not playtime." Wolf seemed to disagree. He charged at Ben, stopping abruptly a few feet away. Rump up, front paws splayed out, telling Ben he wanted to play. Ben relented and tossed a few snowballs at him. At first, they caught Wolf by surprise. Then he chased after them, digging and rolling in the snow wherever they hit. Ben laughed and chased after Wolf. Dodging and leaping, Wolf evaded him easily. Ben was no match.

Breathing hard, Ben stopped to rest and Wolf came over for a pet. "Last night I was worried about you," Ben said, scratching Wolf under his chin. Wolf groaned and wiggled. "I thought you might get mixed up with that pack again. They weren't too friendly to you at the moose kill. I'm glad you came home." He gave Wolf a final scratch and stood up. "I know you're all charged up from the snow, but I've got work to do. Got to make snowshoes to get around in this stuff."

"Grandpa had a pair of snowshoes I played with as a kid. Looks like I'm going to need my own pair now." Ben scratched some tentative patterns in the dirt, trying to recall the details of the snowshoes. "Hmm. . . that's a little short and narrow. Grandpa's were three or four feet long, maybe a foot or more wide." Ben erased parts with his foot and adjusted the sketch. "There. That looks about right."

Curious, Wolf came over and smelled the sketch. Laughing, Ben scratched Wolf's head. "No, I'm not digging mice."

Ben thought the construction details out. "I'll use birch. I've got pieces left over from bow making. About the right size. I'll shape the frames, then bend them, tie the ends together and lace the frame." Easier said than done.

"Let's get on with it." Ben touched up his knife on the sharpening stone and began stripping off the bark on a piece of birch. It peeled off in long white strips. Ben worked all morning on the various pieces. The birch gave off a spicy-sweet smell. Wolf smelled a piece and wrinkled his nose.

Ben roughed out two frame pieces, cut them to size and finished the shaping with his knife. Sighting down the pieces, he said, "They look about right. Now comes the hard part." Ben grasped a piece at both ends and began to pull them together to form the frame. At first the birch bent. Ben applied more pressure. As he closed the "U," the birch snapped. So did Ben's temper. "Damn it!" he yelled, slamming the broken pieces to the floor. Startled, Wolf leaped up from his place by the fire.

"I'm O.K.," he assured Wolf. "Just ticked off. That took hours." Ben picked up a broken piece and studied it, trying to figure out a better way to bend it. "Maybe I don't have to," he murmured. "What if I just notched the ends and tied them together?" Sighing, Ben cut off the damaged wood and started again. He notched the ends of each piece, overlapped them and lashed the ends together with hide straps.

"So far, so good."

Ben cut a crosspiece and fitted it near the front of the frame, then pulled the back ends together to form a taper, trying several positions until it looked right. He secured the two end pieces, then positioned the back crosspiece and tied it to the frame. Ben held the frame up and inspected it.

"Now that looks like a snowshoe. I'm halfway there."

The lacing took more time and Ben worked late into the night finishing the first shoe. The next morning he finished the other one. For a binding Ben made a toe piece out of a wide strip of moose hide, and a strap for the heel. He tried the snowshoes on, adjusting the bindings until they fit right. Ben felt a rush of pride as he finished the shoes. "Well, maybe they're not as pretty as Grandpa's Tahltan snowshoes with the red tassels. Mine are a little crude, but I think they'll do the job."

"Wolf, let's give them a try." Outside, he strapped on the snowshoes and started off in an awkward straddle gait, trying to keep his snowshoes apart. "This can't be right. I feel like a bowlegged cowboy!" Next, he tried shuffling. But when he accidentally dug in the tip of one of the shoes, he got dumped. Wolf stared at Ben. "Don't look at me like I'm an idiot. You don't need snowshoes. You were born with them."

Ben tried again and got the back ends of the shoes crossed, pitching him into the snow. He righted himself again. Then he carefully lifted one shoe up and slid it above the edge of the other shoe. It seemed to work! Ben did the lifting-sliding walk along the edge of the clearing. Wolf followed, watching Ben's feet. "These are gonna to be O.K., Wolf. I think I'm kinda getting the hang of it now."

Later, drying off by the fire, Ben made sketches of a sled in the dirt. He needed something to haul firewood on. The basic bending and lashing techniques would be about the same as he'd used in the snowshoe construction.

The next morning, Ben snowshoed to the stand of birch, where he cut down two trees about the same size. As he cut and limbed them, Wolf started to wander off. Ben called him back. Ruffing his fur, Ben said, "Stay close. I need my grizzly alarm. If the bear catches me off-guard, I won't stand a snowball's chance in hell."

Back at the fire, Ben began shaping the birch into runners. He worked steadily, stopping only to eat and sharpen the axe. By late afternoon, he had shaped the poles into ski-like runners. The next day, he lashed the crosspieces in place. He then rigged a harness out of hide to pull the sled with. Anxious to try it out, he took it outside and pulled it through the snow. "It's nothing fancy, but it works fine. At least it'll carry lots of wood."

Ben loaded his heavy bow, light bow, packsack, axe, and saw onto the sled. Wolf perked up, ready to head out. "Before we do any serious wood cutting, let's make a short trip along our ridge to see what's around in the way of fresh meat. Might scare up a rabbit or two. Maybe something bigger. Grandfather said after the first big snow, animals move around."

Ben left the sled by the lodgepole pines and started scouting the ridge for sign. He had gone only a short distance when hundreds of ptarmigans flushed around him in white waves making clucking-whirring noises. The snow seemed to be moving. "Wow! I've never seen anything like this before," Ben exclaimed. "I've seen ptarmigan around Wrangell, but this is something else."

"Let's get our dinner." With his light bow, Ben took four birds before the flock flew off. He followed the birds up the ridge and shot three more. The ptarmigan flushed again in noisy, undulating waves and disappeared over the ridge. "They're pretty spooked. Not much use to chase them."

Wolf loped up with blood and feathers on his muzzle. "Jeez, Wolf, you're a mess. Let me clean you off." Ben picked off the feathers. Licking his chops, Wolf looked at the ridge, then at Ben. "That's it for today. We still have wood to cut, remember? Besides, those birds are long gone."

Dejected, tail down, Wolf followed Ben back to the sled. Ben stuffed the birds into the pack and started cutting wood. Suddenly, Wolf stiffened and barked a warning. Ears pointed, ruff up, Wolf stared at the clearing, a low rumbling growl in his throat.

# CHAPTER 27

**Alarm signals sounded in Ben's** head. Fitting an arrow, he searched the edge of the clearing and found the grizzly's tracks—the crippled foot tracks perfectly outlined in the snow. The bear's trail followed the edge of the cliffs heading toward the cave. On fear-numbed legs, Ben eased into the clearing. The tracks led straight into the cave.

"Oh God, he's inside." Despair fell over Ben like a dark cloud. "I thought I was going to make it. Everything was going great." Wolf rubbed up against him. Kneeling down next to him, Ben whispered to Wolf. "Things don't look good. We can't stay out here. We've got to get to the cabin." Wolf stared at Ben and then at the cave. "Yeah, it's a screwed-up deal."

Ben stopped at the sled, grabbed the axe and saw and stuffed them into the pack with the birds. "Can't pull the sled with us. It'll just slow us down. Let's go." The wind picked up, blowing snow. By the time they arrived at the cabin, it was dark. "I got to get some heat in this place." From the pack, he took out his flint, tinder, shavings, and kindling. Fire-making had become routine for Ben, and he soon had a fire going. He was grateful the prospector had stocked the cabin with wood. Ben huddled next to the fire, Wolf curled next to him.

Ben awoke the next morning to a cold cabin. The fire had burned down, but not out. He threw some fresh wood on, then stepped outside. A cold wind swirled around him, ice particles stinging his face and hands. Branches swayed and creaked. Grey clouds hung over the valley, pregnant with more snow. A low keening sound filled the air. Shivering, Ben stepped back into the cabin. "Looks like a storm's moving in. Just what we need. Like we don't have enough problems."

Ben gave Wolf a grouse, then skinned one for himself. He skewered his bird on a stick and hung it over the fire. As the bird cooked, drippings flared and popped as they hit the flames and the familiar odors filled the cabin. But cooking sounds and smells failed to comfort Ben as they usually did. The chances of him surviving after losing the cave and all his food, in the middle of winter . . . the prospect left him without hope.

Ben ate in silence, sucking the bones clean. Wolf watched him. "Sorry, Boy. You had yours." He wiped his hands on his coat, then picked up the axe and felt the edge with his thumb. "We're going to need more wood. Lots more wood. Let's do it."

Discouraged, Ben made his way up the bench near John's grave to a stand of lodgepole pine he remembered. He cut and limbed two trees, dragged a log back to the cabin and chopped it into sections. "Winds seem to be picking up," he said to Wolf as they returned to the pine stand for the rest of the wood. Between chops he heard a soft "woof"—not Wolf's grizzly alarm bark, but a bark he'd never heard before.

Puzzled, Ben turned to Wolf. "What's wrong?" Ears cocked, Wolf looked up the valley. Ben scanned the area as far as he could see. "I don't see anything. What's spooking you."

With one final look, Ben began hauling another log toward the cabin.

"Woof."

Wolf looked at Ben and then up the valley, his ears alert, listening.

"Wolf! There's nothing out there. You're giving me the willies." Doubt nagged at Ben. *It's not the grizzly*, he reasoned. *Not that bark*. But fear pressed on his chest.

"Woof."

"Will you knock it off?"

Then he heard it. A distant rumbling. Heart racing, Ben turned and looked up the valley. A noise like a freight train roared out of the south.

**The howling wind bulldozed a** wall of snow before it. Gusting winds knocked Ben over. He jumped up and tried to run toward the cabin. The storm slammed him down into the snow again. Winds screeched and whistled. Ben hugged the snow. *I gotta think. Gotta get a grip. My axe! I can't make it without it.* Panicky, he groped around in the snow until his hand closed on the handle. *Got it!* He reached under his belt and grabbed his gloves and slipped them on. *Can't let my hands freeze.*

Suddenly, the gusts stopped.

In a hunched over, snowshoe-run, Ben tried for the cabin. A curtain of white hung over the valley. Ben couldn't see, but he ran forward blindly. *I should be there by now.* Fear pressed on his chest and throat. He fought to keep the panic down. *If I miss it, I'm dead.* After a few minutes, Ben began to feel the biting cold through his coat.

*It's gotta be just ahead.* Ben bumped into a tree. Fingering the bark, he could feel the deep grooves and knew it was a cottonwood. *No cottonwood trees around the cabin. I'm lost! Let me think. There are cottonwoods down by the river, but how did I miss the cabin?* Ben moved to the other side of the tree to get out of the wind and sat with his back to it. The storm raged around him, blowing through the holes in his coat and chilling him to the core. He rubbed his arms and legs trying to keep warm. The temperature kept dropping. His efforts to keep warmth no longer helped. *I'm not going to make it, Mom. Sorry to do this to you.*

Ben felt strangely detached from the storm. The kid huddled next to the tree was a stranger. Ben had already accepted the inevitable when a shape came out of the storm and nudged him. He didn't respond. Wolf pushed him again, but still Ben didn't move. Insistent, Wolf grabbed Ben by the sleeve and pulled him into the snow.

Confused, Ben struggled to get up. "Wolf? Is that really you? God it's cold." Ben hugged Wolf, feeling his warmth. Wolf pressed up against him and started moving. "Don't go Wolf!" Desperate not to be left alone again, Ben stood, not sure if he wanted to follow Wolf into the blinding whiteness. Wolf grabbed Ben by the sleeve again and tugged. Still disoriented, Ben didn't know what Wolf was doing. Wolf tugged again. Finally, Ben thought he understood. *He's trying to lead me to the cabin.*

"I got it! I got it!" Ben yelled. With one hand on Wolf, he stepped back into the raging storm. It seemed to Ben they walked forever in the snow. Then he stumbled into something. At first, Ben thought he had walked into another tree. He ran his hand over it. Logs. The cabin!

Relief poured over him. Ben groped his way along the wall until he found the door. Jerking it open, he fell inside. Wolf jumped on him, licking Ben in the face. "Easy boy," Ben said, hugging Wolf. Gently, he pushed Wolf down and closed the door. "Let me get some heat in here. I'm frozen."

Ben picked up pieces of pitchy wood and threw them on the coals. Snapping and popping, the fire roared to life. "I never thought I'd hear that sound again," he said, kneeling next to Wolf, stroking his fur. "You saved my tail out there. I'd given up. Don't know how you found your way back to the cabin. But you did."

The storm raged with a fury again. Shrieking winds pounded the cabin, shaking logs loose. The whole cabin shifted suddenly. Wolf bolted up, looking anxiously at the door. "Easy boy, easy," Ben said, consoling Wolf. "Not a lot we can do about it."

Snow blew through cracks in the walls and roof, forming drifts on the dirt floor. Ben huddled next to the fire, keeping it small to conserve wood. He would never survive going out in the storm again.

The cabin creaked and groaned. Wolf paced back and forth in front of the door. "I don't like it either. This place could go any time. Might be smart to get the gear together." Picking up his packsack, Ben stuck the quiver, axe, saw, and snowshoes in the pack and placed it along with the bow next to the door.

As Ben turned to check if he had missed anything, a violent gust battered the cabin. Tearing and splintering, the roof began to buckle. Startled, Wolf jumped up. Ben grabbed the pack and bow, kicked the door open, and jumped clear, Wolf leaping after him. With a final snapping and shattering of timbers, the roof caved in. Snow poured into the cabin.

The blizzard caught them full force. Feeling his way along the wall, Ben got on the lee side of the cabin. With his snowshoes and axe, he dug a shallow snow cave that butted up against the cabin wall. Crawling in, Ben sat with his back against the logs. Wolf curled up with his head under his tail, next to Ben. They spent a long, sleepless night huddled in the snow cave, shivering, and listening to the storm roar around them. Ben wasn't sure they'd make it through another day without shelter or a fire.

But the next the morning the howling winds stopped abruptly. Ben couldn't believe his ears. "God, could it possibly be over? Let's see what's out there."

Ben crawled out behind Wolf and encountered a white wilderness. Snow blanketed the country, forming deep drifts. In some places, only the tops of the trees showed above the snow. An ominous silence hung over the valley. Not a sign of life. Numbed, Ben stood without speaking.

Wolf stood pressed against Ben. Lifting his muzzle, he howled. The full-throated wail split the silence, rising and undulating in intensity and pitch, then dropping to a series of moans. The wild call filled the stillness. A medley of howls, yelps and cries answered. Ben felt the despair in the plaintive cries. "Sounds to me like the pack's in trouble too."

"Wolf, we're going back to the cave. I'm done in. We can't make it out here. Grandpa told me grizzlies change dens during the winter. Maybe the bear's gone. Maybe not. But we're outta food and outta choices. I don't even have the energy to hunt."

Ben shouldered the pack and started up the valley, mechanically working his snowshoes through the snow. Approaching the cave, he stopped at the edge of the clearing. Drifts covered the entrance to the cave. Ben could see no tracks. "I think he's still in there."

Overwhelmed by the situation, Ben slumped down next to a tree, anger building up. *How much of this crap do I have to take? I haven't eaten for days, I'm freezing my tail off. And every time we turn around we get screwed. I've had it!*

Ben stood up and brushed the snow off his coat. "I'm tired of running, Wolf. Let's take our cave back."

# CHAPTER 29

**From the edge of the woods**, Ben studied the cliff. The wind had blown the snow off the lookout, forming thirty foot drifts at the base of the cliff. "Wolf, I've got an idea."

Ben broke trail along the edge of the clearing to the stand of lodgepole pine. The exertion and the cold sapped his strength, but desperation kept him going. With the saw he cut dead and near-dead boughs. He had started fires with them before and knew they burned like gasoline.

Ben then cut off live branches and tied them together. He paused several times afraid the grizzly could hear him sawing. He hoped the snow in the cave entrance would dampen the sound. Deciding he had enough, Ben loaded the packsack and started up the drift. Kicking the toes of his snowshoes into the snow, he cut out "steps" and climbed up to the smoke hole, Wolf by his side.

Ben brushed the snow away next to the hole, then took off his gloves and prepared a fire. From the pack, he took out fire-making materials. He wadded up the tinder into a ball and arranged kindling over it, then he piled up the dead boughs until they reached his waist. Last, he put the green boughs on top.

As he kneeled to start the fire, Ben heard Wolf snarl. "No, Wolf! Don't." From below, inside the cave, came an answering growl. "Oh God, now the bear knows we're up here." Grabbing his bow and quiver, Ben ran over to the edge of the lookout. He jerked out an arrow and fitted it to his bowstring.

*I may have a chance for a second shot.* He aimed at the cave entrance and drew the bow. Wolf watched the bear through the smoke hole, his ears erect, lips curled, ruff up. *You seem to be keeping him busy. Maybe I can still get the fire going.*

Ben leaned the bow and arrow against a rock and raced back to the stack of boughs. Hunching down, Ben struck the flint, but his cold hands dropped the knife. "Settle down," he told himself. He rubbed his hands together to warm them, then hit the flint again. A spray of weak sparks flared and died. He repositioned the flint, but this time struck it at the wrong angle and the few scattered sparks missed their mark. "Get with it, kid."

The huffing and clacking of teeth grew louder.

"Come on. Come on." Ben breathed a silent prayer and struck the flint again, sending shower of sparks into the tinder. This time glowing spots appeared. But Ben blew too hard and put the sparks out.

Desperate, Ben struck the flint again and again with shaking hands. *This has to work. It has to!* At last a stream of sparks shot into the tinder. Gently, he picked it up and blew on the tinder. Red spots grew, then fluttered into a tiny flame. Ben gave a sigh of relief. Carefully, he slid the tinder back under the kindling. A small blue-yellow flame licked at the bark, then flared, sweeping up into the boughs. Immediately, the bundles exploded into a hot crackling fire.

Ben nudged Wolf aside and peered down into the cave. The grizzly reared up, working his jaw and slobbering, his face just below the hole. He reached out a claw, trying to grab at Ben. Jumping back, Ben kicked the fire into the hole. A stream of flaming debris poured down on the bear.

There was a roar. Then the grizzly exploded out of the cave, fur smoking, and rolled in the snow. Ben grabbed his bow and released an arrow, hitting the grizzly high in the shoulder. With a savage bite at the wound, the bear snapped off the shaft. Shooting again, Ben hit the bear in the flank. The grizzly turned and crashed into the brush at the edge of the clearing.

"It's get-even time, bear!" Ben yelled. Seconds later he could see the grizzly emerge from the timber still running and bound away down the valley.

Charged up with adrenalin, full of fight, Ben grabbed the pack, pointed his snowshoes downhill and slid off the lookout. Down in the clearing, Ben stared grim-faced at the spot in the brush where the grizzly had fled. "Wolf, I put two arrows in him! I did it! *This is our place,* we took it back, and it feels good!"

Pushing through the snow, Ben entered the cave. The door lay on the floor, part of the wall had been knocked over. The rank, musty smell of bear overwhelmed everything. The ladder had been knocked over. He lifted it into position, raced up the ladder to the meat cache, grabbed a handful jerky and threw it down to Wolf. Snatching more, Ben gulped the meat.

"O.K.," he said between bites, "let's get a fire going. That animal could come back anytime." Ben built a fire right in the entrance, then kindled a cooking fire. With two fires going, things looked brighter.

Ben scooped a coffee pot full of snow and put it on the fire. As the water got hot, he put a handful of jerky in it. When the meat boiled, Ben poured off the broth. The hot soup tasted like heaven. He drank the full pot, finishing with the meat. Groaning with pleasure, he said, "This has gotta be the best eating I've ever had. And for the first time in a week I'm full. I'm warm. I'm safe."

Suddenly, the victory high wore off, leaving Ben feeling tired and used up. He wrestled the door out of the snow and slid it back into place. The bear had rearranged the bed too, raking it up into a pile. But the hide was intact. Ben salvaged what he could of the mattress boughs, then crawled into bed and pulled the hide over him. He instantly fell into a deep sleep. With his head resting on his forelegs, Wolf watched the entrance.

The next morning, Ben cautiously exited the cave, watching Wolf. Wolf lifted his muzzle to the breeze, but didn't alert. Satisfied the grizzly wasn't near, Ben studied the entrance. "We've got to bear-proof the cave someway. That grizzly's coming back. If he catches us inside, we're history." Ben looked around for anything that could stand up to the grizzly. "There's got to be a way . . . log wall maybe . . . don't have time . . . keep a fire going?"

Ben shook his head in frustration. His chest and throat tightened with fear. He gave up and turned to go back into the cave. Then he stopped. The slab! He looked up at the refrigerator-sized hunk of granite that perched over the entrance. "That's it. I've got to drop the slab over the entrance. Even the grizzly couldn't move that thing. And if it doesn't work . . ."

But Ben didn't finish. Instead he began climbing. When he and Wolf reached the slab, he examined it carefully. Over the years, it had worked its way down the side of the cliff face, resting on the edge immediately above the cave entrance. "With a little help this thing might go, Wolf." Ben crawled out on the rock and looked down at the cave opening, trying to visualize how the slab would fall.

"I'm going to give it a try." He cleaned around the rock, then bracing his back against a nearby boulder, Ben pushed the slab with his feet. "Move, damn it! Move!" Nothing. He changed positions and tried again. "No! That's not going to do it. It's probably frozen." He thought for a minute. "Maybe a pry of some sort?"

Near the cave, Ben cut and trimmed a birch, working quickly, afraid the grizzly would return. "Keep alert, Wolf. That bear's around here someplace."

"O.K., let's do it." Ben dragged the birch pole up to the slab and levered one end under it. Using the other boulder as a fulcrum, Ben applied his full weight. "Move rock, move!" When it didn't budge, he tried bouncing on the pole. Still nothing. Repositioning the pole, Ben tried again and again. The slab wouldn't move.

Frustrated, Ben sat on the boulder and pictured in his mind how to move the rock. "Maybe if I gave the boulder a little more height." He found a flat rock and straining, he muscled it on top of the boulder, then he worked the pole back under the slab.

"One more time," he muttered, leaning his full weight on the pole. There was a grating sound as the slab moved an inch, then abruptly stopped. "Come on rock, go!" Ben shook his head in frustration. He pulled the pole out about a foot and tried again. "Now, do it!" *Creak! Creak! Creak!* Ben bounced on the pole. Suddenly, the slab broke free and crashed over the side, spilling snow and debris in front of the cave. Ben toppled down into the snow.

He scrambled over to the edge and threw up his hands in frustration. "No! I screwed it up . . . blocked the entrance!" Heart racing, Ben slid down the ledge and inspected the slab. It covered the entire entrance except for a narrow opening. Ben worked his arm and shoulder into the gap, but could go no further. "No way I'm going to get into the cave this way." Frustrated, he stared at the slab.

Wolf came over and nuzzled him. "I've got to fix it, Wolf. We're dead meat out here. We might be able to get down through the smoke hole, but we'd have to make a ladder and that takes time. Time we don't have. I've got me a bad feeling about that bear." Ben searched the clearing and listened for alarm calls. "Anything out there?" Wolf wagged his tail. *If he's downwind you can't smell him.* Ben thought.

"I've got to open up that entrance more." Ben climbed back up and pushed the pole over the side. Sliding off the ledge, Ben inspected the slab again. At the top it tilted slightly to the right. He positioned the pole between the cave opening and the top edge of the slab. Straining, he pushed, feeling movement. "That's it. Come on. Move! Move! Move!"

Slowly, the slab moved over and stopped. Ben caught his breath. "I think we did it. Let's try it for size." Wolf ran easily through the opening. Ben had to squeeze through sideways. "Grizzly's not going to get by that hunk of granite. It probably weighs half a ton. Wolf, we now have us a bear-proof cave!" Wagging his tail, Wolf headed toward his sleeping spot.

Suddenly changing his course, Wolf barked a warning and leaped at the opening. The grizzly charged the entrance, struggling to get past the slab. Slobbering and huffing, the bear stuck his head through the opening and roared. The savage, primeval sound filled the cave.

Wolf attacked, slashing at the bear's head. Reacting, Ben grabbed his spear and thrust at toward the bear. The tip glanced off the boney forehead. Thrusting again, Ben stabbed the grizzly's nose. Grunting with pain, the bear backed out. Ben could hear him snorting and clacking his teeth as he retreated in pain.

Angry with himself, Ben waited with spear ready. "I screwed up, Wolf. Screwed up royally. I should've stuck him in the throat when I had the chance." Ruff up, teeth bared, Wolf watched the entrance, pacing back and forth.

"Easy, he's still out there. We're going to stay put for a while. This might be in his den or he might just be trying to kill me for some other reason. Either way I lose."

Ben sat by the fire unable to sleep. *I came within minutes of dying today. That bear nearly caught me outside.*

# CHAPTER 30

**After the attack, Ben stayed** in the cave, afraid to leave. There was no doubt in his mind that the grizzly was stalking him. After several days without a fire, Ben's patience snapped. "Wolf, I've had it! I'm tired of freezing our butts off. I'm tired of eating cold food. I've burned the smoking racks and my mattress, but I'll be damned if I'll burn my chair and ladder. Enough is enough! Let's get some wood."

Ben peered out the entrance, checked the clearing and listened for birds. "I don't see or hear anything out there, Wolf. Looks O.K., but stay close." Body poised for flight, pulse pounding, Ben left the cave armed with his bow and spear. Grizzly tracks criss-crossed the snow around the entrance to the cave. Ben could read the grizzly's frustration in the maze of tracks. He skirted the edge of the clearing until he found where the tracks led down toward the valley. Watchful, he followed the grizzly's trail to make sure he hadn't circled back.

"Wolf, I think he's gone. Let's cut some wood." Ben worked feverishly.

The wind changed.

Wolf barked.

A thousand pounds of grey death erupted from the edge of the timber, charging Ben in long bounding leaps. Kicking off his snowshoes, spear in hand, Ben pulled himself up a tree limb. The grizzly swiped at Ben, a paw raking his boot. Grabbing for a higher branch, Ben dropped the spear. Powerful jaws clamped on his coat, jerking Ben out of the tree.

Wolf attacked with his teeth, tearing and slashing at the grizzly's back legs. Hampered by the deep snow, Ben struggled to get to his feet. Six-inch claws slapped at his head. He fell against the tree, blood pouring down his face. Charging the bear, Wolf attacked and retreated. The grizzly grabbed Ben again, closing massive jaws on his shoulder.

Leaping on the grizzly's back, Wolf sank his teeth into the bear's neck. The grizzly reared up and threw Wolf off. Ben staggered to his feet. Blinded by blood, he felt for a limb and pulled himself up into the tree. Slipping, he grabbed desperately for a solid hold. The grizzly charged again, smashing into the tree.

Claws ripped into Ben's boot. Jerking his legs up, Ben fought to stay in the tree. He kicked out blindly and hit the grizzly's nose. Grunting in pain, the bear opened his jaws. As Ben pulled himself up the tree, his hand closed on the spear, which had lodged in the crook of a branch.

Below, Wolf darted in and out slashing at the grizzly's hindquarters. The bear spun around and swiped at Wolf, who dodged and retreated. In a rage, the grizzly reared up to get at Ben, his giant head just inches from Ben's battered body. Wiping the blood from his eyes and steadying himself, Ben drove the spear into the bear's throat, burying the twelve-inch blade to the hilt.

Slapping at the spear, the grizzly snapped the shaft; blood spurting from his throat. Enraged, the bear lunged at the tree, snarling a bloody foam. Ruff up and growling, Wolf attacked again.

Swinging around, the grizzly swiped at Wolf, knocking him into the snow. Then he turned back to the tree, biting and tearing off hunks of bark and wood. Chomping his jaws, the bear struggled to get at Ben. A steady stream of arterial blood pumped from the grizzly's throat, turning the snow crimson. Ben could smell the musty-sweet odor of blood.

Beginning to weaken, the bear dropped to the ground. Ben climbed higher. Lunging up, the grizzly stared at Ben. Ben wiped the blood from his eyes, and their eyes met. He no longer saw rage; he saw acceptance of death. The bear dropped down on his feet and collapsed. Lifting his head, the animal attempted to rise. Then he lay still. Cautiously, Wolf approached the grizzly, sniffing at him. Dazed, Ben hung in the tree, afraid to move, blood streaming down his face and shoulders.

Wolf stood next to the bear, gazing up at Ben. Realizing the grizzly was dead, Ben eased down from the tree. Picking up a handful of snow, he wiped his face, the snow came away in a red mush. He stared at the bloody snow in disbelief. Gingerly, he traced the wound on his forehead with his fingers. The scalp was torn from his right temple to over his left eye. Scooping up another handful of snow, he wiped the blood from his eyes.

"I'm hurt! Hurt bad!" Ben cried out in pain.

# CHAPTER 31

Confused, Ben struggled into his snowshoes and staggered down the ridge, going the wrong way. Wolf nudged him toward the cave. Ben walked in a daze, not knowing where he was heading. Wolf got in front of him and turned him toward the cave again. As the shock began wearing off Ben felt a searing fire across his forehead. By the time he reached the cave, his head and shoulder throbbed with an intense, burning pain. "Gotta lie down." Crawling into bed, Ben passed out. Wolf laid his head on Ben's thigh, watching him.

Late in the day, Ben awoke. As soon as he opened his eyes, Wolf jumped up, head cocked, ears alert, examining Ben. Woofing and wagging his tail, Wolf nudged him to get him out of bed. "I'm not feeling too sharp."

Dragging himself up, Ben steadied himself against the wall The room spun around him. He slumped back down on the bed feeling weaker than he ever had in his life. Wolf rubbed up against him, whining and pushing his muzzle into Ben's hand. He could barely pet him, his head felt like it was on fire. Moving slowly, he went outside and piled snow on his scalp. The cold relieved enough of the pain that he crawled back into bed, Wolf at his side.

Early the next morning Ben got up, built the fire and put water on to heat for tea and broth. He climbed up the ladder, stopping several times, still a unsure on his feet. He threw down jerky for Wolf.

After a handful of jerky and a cup of rose hip tea, Ben said, "I've been putting it off. It's time to look at the damage." Carefully, Ben ran his fingers along the scalp wound. The tear was still oozing blood. Feeling empty of emotion, he found the shaving mirror and examined his forehead. His scalp had been torn loose. A jagged rip ran from his right temple to just above his left eye. An angry, blood-crusted ridge had formed at the edges of the tear.

It was too much to wrap his mind around, so Ben moved on to his other injuries. He removed his coat and shirt and studied his shoulder. The caribou skin had saved him there. With a better grip, the grizzly's massive jaws would have crushed his shoulder, but the bear had grabbed the loose hide. As it was, the bear's teeth had gouged out Ben's skin in three ragged chunks. "Looks bad, but not too bad. Gotta be cleaned, but with what? I don't need an infection." Then he remembered the prospector's whiskey. He found the bottle, uncorked it and poured whiskey onto the torn flesh of his shoulder, screaming out at the shock of it. When the pain subsided, he put his shirt back on.

"The other's still gotta be done," Ben said, looking into the shaving mirror again. He ran his fingers along his bloody scalp. "I've got to sew my hair back on. And it's probably gonna hurt like hell." Ben found a niche in the wall at eye level where he could prop the mirror. The light was dim, so Ben built up the fire using pitch-streaked pine to make it burn brighter. He lit a few candles for even more light, placing them next to the mirror. Then Ben threaded the needle with fishing line and sterilized it with whiskey. Carefully, he lifted up the blood-crusted scalp and poured the whiskey on the wound.

He thought his head would explode. Feeling himself going faint, Ben sat down until the wave of nausea and dizziness passed. Then he lifted the flap of his scalp, gritted his teeth, and poured whiskey on the open wound a second time. Groaning with pain, Ben fought to stay conscious. Wolf nudged him, whining. "I'm hurting . . . don't know if I can do it."

Ben leaned against the wall, working up his courage, then stood up, resolved. "It's time!" Looking in the mirror, he squeezed the scalp and skin together with his left hand. Ben took a deep breath and started the first stitch just behind his right ear. It was awkward trying to hold the skin and scalp together while also pushing the needle through both layers. He made several attempts before he tied off the stitch, his fingers slippery with blood.

"Oh, man, this hurts!" He sat down until the pain subsided a bit. Then he worked up his courage and made several more stitches as quickly as he could. Hurting, he got another handful of snow and held it against his forehead. "You gotta finish it, Ben." He tried again, spacing the stitches about half an inch apart. Each time he drove the needle through his skin, nausea rose up in his throat. After a few more minutes, he stopped and sat down to let the pain ease.

"I can't do it anymore, Wolf. That's it. I can't handle this." He went outside and scooped more snow onto his hairline. He fingered the stitches and the loose piece of scalp. "Huh. I'm just about finished. Might as well get it over with." He braced himself against the pain and pushed the needle through the skin, wincing each time. Finally, Ben tied off the last stitch slightly past his left eye. He had pierced his forehead and scalp fifteen times.

Ben collapsed into an exhausted sleep.

The next morning, Ben felt a tightness where he had sewn the scalp, but the pain seemed to be going away. Looking in the mirror, he traced the stitches with his fingers. "Looks like it's gonna hold," Ben said, feeling proud of his handiwork. He built up the fire and heated water for rose hip tea. The cracking and popping of the wood cheered him. "Didn't think I was going to make it for awhile."

Ben removed his shirt and examined his shoulder. The teeth marks looked red and angry and had started to scab over, but he didn't see any puss. "Doesn't look infected." In the first aid kit, Ben found iodine and poured it on the wounds, just in case. He used band-aids to cover the gouges. Ben sighed with relief.

Then he noticed Wolf licking his fur. "What's wrong, Boy? Let's take a look." Looking closer Ben saw the blood Wolf was trying to lick away. "I'm sorry, Wolf. I've been so out of it I didn't even notice." Shaking his head, Ben traced the six-inch gash with his finger. "You got a bad cut there. Looks like he got a claw into you. It's gotta be sewed. It's going to hurt." Ben looked into

Wolf's trusting eyes.

"I don't need this."

Ben threaded the needle and sterilized it and the fishing line. He talked to Wolf in soothing a tone. "Sorry, Wolf. Don't know how you're gonna take this, but I've got to do it."

He let Wolf smell the whiskey. Then Ben poured it on the wound. Flinching, Wolf began licking it. Ben stroked Wolf and talked to him in the same soft, soothing tone as he tried to make a stitch. Wolf nosed Ben's hands away and stared at him. Ben tried several more times, but Wolf became more agitated, finally moving away from Ben.

"God, I hate this. There's no way to put you out like a vet would. Let me think." From a piece of caribou skin, Ben cut several long strips. Lifting Wolf's front legs, Ben tied two half hitches around them. Trusting Ben, Wolf slumped to his knees. Ben stroked Wolf until he settled down, then he slipped two loops of hide straps over the Wolf's jaws and tightened the rope. Struggling to get free, Wolf got up on his hind legs. Wrestling him to the ground, Ben tied off the back legs. Wolf was immobile. "Sorry, Fella." Ben said, looking into Wolf's frightened and confused eyes. "It's gotta be done."

Wolf flinched as Ben poured the remainder of the whiskey on the wound. Talking softly, Ben tried to stitch up the wound again. Each time he pierced Wolf's hide, it would quiver. The piteous whining was almost more than Ben could take. He thought he was going to be sick. Finally, he tied off the last stitch.

"It's all right. I'm finished now," Ben said, removing the straps from the legs. Wolf lurched up. The ticklish part was removing the half hitches from Wolf's jaws. He didn't know how Wolf would react. "Easy now. I'm trying to help you." As he loosened the strap, Ben jumped back. Wolf looked into Ben's eyes, then leaped through the cave entrance. Ben ran after him, calling his name. He waited up most of the night, but Wolf was gone.

The next morning Ben awoke to a lonely cave. He had left the door open, hoping Wolf would return. Disappointed, he climbed to the lookout and searched the valley, but there was no sign of Wolf. The stark landscape stretched before Ben as far as he could see. Snow clouds hung on the horizon. From the upper valley, a cold breeze flowed down, carrying with it the smell of snow.

Ben felt empty and lonely, but life went on. The bear hide needed to be taken take care of. He knew he couldn't waste it. He had made a promise. As he approached the grizzly, he flushed the scavenger birds. They fluttered off, landing a few yards from the kill. The bear lay next to the tree, sprawled on his back in a pool of frozen blood. Dried blood matted the bear's throat and upper body. His jaw, set in a death grin, showed yellow teeth. Birds had eaten his tongue and plucked out his eyes. Blood stained the snow where he and Wolf had fought the grizzly. From the tracks, he could see how Wolf attacked and harassed the grizzly. He looked at his own blood spattered on the cottonwood.

Ben stood strangely detached from the scene. Somehow it was all unreal.

It was over; he was alive. Ben pulled out the broken shaft of the spear and examined the blade, feeling the edge with thumb. "It did it's job."

Laying the spear aside, Ben took off his mittens and started skinning out the grizzly. The animal smelled of death. He cut his arrowhead out of the shoulder. "Didn't do much damage. Should have put it in the lungs." He couldn't find the other arrow. Near the ribs, Ben noticed a hard lump. Curious, he probed it with his knife, striking metal. Ben dug out a bullet. "I bet this slug came from John's Winchester. Looks like you got off a shot, John."

Skinning the bear proved to be a long and cold job. Ben stopped several times to warm his hands. He skinned out each side and under the grizzly's back as far as he could reach. Ben stood up, eyeing the bear. "Hootz, you're too heavy to turn over." He thought for a minute. "With a little help from gravity, I think I can do it."

Ben retrieved the shovel from the cave. He dug under the bear on the downhill side. The snow gave way, rolling the grizzly over on his stomach. Soon, Ben finished skinning out the grizzly, then dragged the heavy hide to the sled, and muscled it on. Breathing hard, Ben muttered, "That hide must've weighed a hundred pounds."

"Hootz, I've heard stories of how the hunters put the head of a bear they killed into a tree so it can watch the sun come up. It's supposed to set the soul free. I will do this for you." Ben cut the grizzly's head off using the saw to get through the spine. On a grassy knoll, Ben found a lone cottonwood tree. Ben wedged the head in a branch, the face looking east. "Hootz, you can see your valley from here." Ben paused, thinking of the hatred he'd seen in those eyes. "I hope your soul is free now, and your angry spirit is at peace. We could have lived the way of the *Kolosh*, but you wouldn't have it."

# CHAPTER 32

Back in the cave, Ben built up the fire, cleared a place next to it, and dragged in the grizzly's hide. With the axe, he began fleshing the hide. The fat rolled off in dirty-grey wads. As it piled up, he shoveled the stinking mess outside, but still the carrion smell filled the cave. The next day, he completed scraping the bear skin. He built a new rack and began smoking the hide. After three days, Ben called it good. With the hide side down, he put it on his bed to use for a blanket.

Loneliness hung heavily on Ben. He missed Wolf. He went through the motions of eating, but the food was tasteless. Wolf had made the situation livable. But Wolf had been gone for over a week. Ben gave up hope that he would ever return. Without him, Ben just tried to fill the hours. Cutting wood took up a good share of his time.

When Ben checked his calendar, he figured it was December, maybe January. He sat in the chair next to the fire thinking about what he should do. *Grandpa said this is the time to get out of here. The rivers are frozen. But it's still two or three hundred miles to the nearest Mountie post through rough country and rough weather. There's a really good chance I might not make it. I've got food and shelter here and I've been written off. No one is looking for me. But if I don't do it now I'll have to wait until the next freeze-up. A year from now . . .*

Tossing a piece of wood on the fire, Ben said, "I'm gonna try for it. But first, I've got to tell Grandpa goodbye."

The next morning, Ben packed the sled. This was the first time since building the sled that Wolf wasn't with him. He missed having Wolf around, hurrying him up. Deep snow covered the upper valley. Ben had trouble recognizing landmarks. As he came up on the lake, he located the grave drifted over with snow. The white birch tree marking the site stood out against the stark winter sky.

*"Ah wa sa,"* Ben said, greeting Grandfather. Head bowed, Ben was silent for a few minutes, feeling the hurt. "I'm going to walk out. Try for Telegraph Creek, like you said. I've been here about six months . . . maybe more." Ben stopped, thinking of how long he had been in the valley. "I kinda lost track of time."

"Dan never made it back. I put all his gear in a tree over there," Ben said, nodding in the direction. "I had to kill Hootz, Grandpa. I had no choice. I told him who I was and my clan, but he wouldn't listen. I honored him in the old way. Hung his head in a tree facing east so his soul could escape, Grandpa. He could see his valley from there."

"I've had a wolf with me, Grandpa. *Dikaanwaawu* must have sent him to me. I think I'm beginning to understand some of the old ways." Ben's eyes brimmed over, "You are the best grandfather a boy could ever have. I won't say goodbye. Our people don't have a word for that. I guess I'll just say I love you."

Ben turned and walked away from Grandfather for the last time.

Back at the cave, Ben prepared to leave. He oiled the Winchester, wrapped it in a piece of moose hide and placed it in the cache. He rolled up the grizzly hide and hung it over the meat rack to keep it away from small creatures. Then Ben cut wood and stacked it next to the fire pit. "Just in case I don't make it out and have to come back."

Then Ben loaded several larger pieces of dry, yellow-streaked lodgepole pine for emergency fires. He couldn't shake Grandfather's words: "At forty below, you do not make mistakes. You'll not get a second chance." He filled John's packsack with dry tinder, kindling, and extra sparking flints, and arranged it on the sled. Then he filled Dan's army packsack with jerky, the frying pan, coffee pot, and a cup and fork, and placed it next to John's pack. Ben lashed every thing down and secured the axe to the top of the load. He was ready to go.

"I'll check the cave one last time." The fire had burned out, leaving the cave cold and lonely. A sadness washed over him. *This has been my home for six months. I put a lot of work in here.* Going over to the shelf, Ben arranged the extra gear he didn't need, the prospector's pick and gold pan, in neat order. He moved John's chair a little closer to the fire place.

He looked at Wolf's spot by the fire, reached down and ran his hand over the depression. He pictured Wolf stretched out in front of him and a sadness descended on him like a dark cloud. "I miss you, Wolf." He walked out of the cave opening and pushed the door closed behind him.

"Wonder if I'll ever see this place again?" Ben said to himself, feeling lonely and apprehensive about leaving. "Time to get going. Grandpa said we were about 250 or so miles away from the Mountie station. With this load, it's going to be one long, hard pull."

# CHAPTER 33

**With a sense of foreboding,** Ben started down the valley pulling the sled. The crusted snow made it easier to travel. He stopped at the cabin site and looked up the valley toward the cave. "I could still go back. I know what's back there but not what's ahead. No, Mom's hurting. She lost Dad and probably thinks she lost me, too. I'll give it a try."

Passing the cabin site, Ben camped in a grove of spruce. As he was hollowing out a snow cave, something nudged him from behind. Startled, Ben whirled around to find a grey face and yellow eyes staring back at him.

"Wolf! You're back. I thought I'd lost you." Ben hugged him. His fur smelled like clean straw. "I'm so glad to see you. I didn't mean to hurt you." Wolf wiggled, making happy sounds. Ben kneeled down and stroked him. "Let me look at your wound." When Ben inspected the wound, Wolf froze but didn't pull back. "Looks good. It's healed, no infection. Your hair even covers the scar."

That night in the snow cave with Wolf curled up next to him, Ben felt some hope.

As Ben left the area he knew behind, his misgivings grew. The wilderness seemed to go on forever with no sign of civilization. Soon, he lost track of the days. Everywhere Ben looked, snow-covered mountains, forests, hills, plateaus, and valleys filled the land. He worried that one of the frozen rivers they crossed was the Stikine. That they had gone too far.

For several days the temperature dropped. Tree sap froze and exploded, sounding like gun shots. Too cold to travel, Ben and Wolf waited out the weather in a snow cave. The unyielding cold and the rigors of the trail sapped all of Ben's strength and most of his hope.

Ben had about reached the end of his endurance when the stream they were following emptied into a larger river. He walked along the bank to get a better view. "It's a big river. Gotta be the Stikine, Wolf."

Cautiously hopeful, Ben picked up the sled rope and started down the frozen river with Wolf at his side. On the third day, just before dusk, Ben smelled wood smoke and heard dogs barking. Looking across the river, he saw weathered log cabins strung along the bluff. From one of the cabins a Canadian flag flapped in the breeze.

Ben couldn't believe his eyes. "Mountie station, Wolf! The Mountie station! We made it!" Ben dropped the sled rope and began running toward the cabins. "Come on, Wolf. Let's see what civilization is like."

Wolf held back, whining softly. "What's the matter?" Wolf nuzzled Ben, but wouldn't go any farther. "What're you trying to tell me?" Gently placing his paws on Ben's shoulders, Wolf licked him and tenderly nibbled his ear. Suddenly, Ben understood: Wolf was saying good-bye. Hugging Wolf, Ben caressed him and talked to him gently. "I couldn't have made it with out you. You saved my life. Don't leave me now. We've got a big yard at home and a park just down the street."

Wolf pulled away from Ben. Dropping to all fours, he loped away through the timber, appearing on a knoll overlooking the river. Ben called out to stop him, but Wolf continued on. At the top of the rise, Wolf lifted his head and howled. The long, mournful sound split the winter sky, a call Ben had never heard before. Answering howls and yelps came from the settlement. For a minute, Wolf stood silhouetted on the hill. Then he turned and disappeared into the wilderness.

Ben ran up the knoll, calling out for Wolf. Then he stopped.

His heart told him: *Wolf is a wild animal. He needs to run free. He would never survive in Seattle.* Loneliness swept over Ben. Getting out no longer seemed important to him. Eyes brimming over, Ben whispered, "Goodbye, Wolf. I'll never forget you." With a heavy heart, Ben started across the frozen river. Lunging at their tethers, the dogs began a frenzied barking. A Mountie stepped out of his cabin, hollering at the dogs. Looking to see what was causing all the commotion, the officer couldn't believe his eyes.

Dressed in skins, his furry ski mask pulled over his face, carrying a long bow and a spear, a quiver of arrows slung over his back, Ben presented a strange sight to the young policeman. Ben could see the look of astonishment on the man's face. Ben pulled back his hood. The policeman peered at him.

"You're the James kid, aren't you?"

Startled, Ben didn't respond. This was the first human voice, other than his own, he had heard in seven months. Finally, Ben found his voice: "Yes, sir. I'm Ben. Ben James."

"And I'm Constable Jack Carruthers, RCMP," the Mountie said, extending his hand. Somewhat dazed, Ben shook it. "We'd given you up for dead months ago. Where are Paul and Taggart? They with you?"

"Grandpa died in June. Probably a heart attack or stroke. Don't know what happened to Dan. We had some engine trouble. Said he was going up for a test hop and never came back."

The Mountie was silent for a minute. "I'm sorry. I knew both of them. They were good men. But don't count Dan out. He's flown the bush since the war. Always carries survival gear with him."

"I saw you fly over last summer. We searched the Tahltan Creek area, but didn't find a trace."

Ben couldn't give anymore details. He was tired, sad, and overwhelmed. Details could wait.

Carruthers picked up the sled rope and turned to Ben, "Don't want to burn dinner, I've got a moose roast about ready to take out of the oven, along with baked potatoes, sourdough biscuits and a dried apple pie." Grinning, he said, "Looks like you could use a good meal," he paused and sniffed, " . . . and a hot bath."

# EPILOGUE

Ben's mother met him in Wrangell. Ben thought she would never stop crying or hugging him, but he didn't mind too much. He became an instant celebrity, interviewed by newspapers and radio stations. He received hundreds of letters, mostly from teenage girls, some as far away as Japan.

Yet Ben felt a strange reluctance to profit from his experience. He couldn't explain it to his mother or even to himself, but he did know that what he had been through was deeply personal, even sacred. It had to do with himself, with Grandfather, with his Tlingit heritage and with Wolf. Ben's seven month ordeal in the wilderness of British Columbia changed him. Physically, he was in the best shape he had ever been. Long hikes and snowshoeing treks, along with wood cutting and daily survival activities, had left Ben with a lean, hard body.

Ben would carry the scars of the grizzly attack all his life. Even though a Seattle plastic surgeon worked on the ragged tear at Ben's scalp line, it never entirely disappeared. On cold winter days, a faint red line would sometimes show. For the most part, his hair covered the scar, but it and the gouges on his shoulder would always remind Ben of the grizzly's fury.

The greatest change in Ben was psychological. He carried himself with a quiet self-assurance he had never had before. He viewed the world differently and his interests changed. When the coach invited him to try out for the team, Ben politely declined. Sports no longer seemed important. He had competed in a life-and-death struggle and won. Ben did work out in a Seattle gym to keep up his boxing skills.

Ben and Jeannie dated a few times, but she was caught up in the high school scene and Ben wasn't. After her sophomore year, Jeannie moved to California. They corresponded for a while, but then the letters stopped. Ben never saw her again. Sometimes he thought of her and wondered what she might be doing.

The June after Ben's return, Constable Carruthers flew him, his mother, and two Tlingit Elders back into the valley. The Elders would prepare Grandfather's body to be taken back to Wrangell. They approached the lake and Ben tensed as they passed over the cliffs and dropped down for a landing. Carruthers taxied the Beaver to shore. Switching off the motor, he looked at Ben with an unasked question. "I'm fine. A little spooked for a minute when we came over the ridge. But I'm fine now." Ben felt his mother's hand on his shoulder.

Ben took the group over to the grave. After the Mountie took pictures and the Elders inspected the grave, they left Ben and his mother alone. She told her father she loved him, then she asked Ben, "Do you want some time alone with your grandfather?" Ben nodded.

Ben stood several minutes in silence, thinking of the events of the past year. Then he explained to Grandfather how the grizzly, the valley, the wolf, and the old ways had changed him, probably forever. Ben reminisced with

Grandfather about family, Wrangell, fish camps, and hunting trips. He assured Grandfather that he would have a traditional funeral and potlatch, and told him he loved him. Ben turned to go. Then he stopped and smiled. "I never nicked your axe, Grandpa. Kept it sharp as a razor."

After the Elders had prepared Grandfather's body for transportation, Ben led the way down the valley and along the cliffs, to the cave. In some ways it was like coming home. Overcome by memories, Ben pushed the door open. When his eyes adjusted, he surveyed the interior. Everything was as he left it. In his mind, Ben could almost see Wolf lying in his spot. Images of him crowded Ben's memory, happy but painful. Sensing his hurt, his mom put her arm around him.

Ben had told her before, but now that they were there, Ben could show his mother how he had fixed up the cave, smoked meat, tanned hides, and made it his home. He took the grizzly skin from the smoking rack and spread it on the floor. "That's the biggest grizzly I've ever seen in these parts," Carruthers said, as he paced off the length. "Eight feet from nose to tail. On his hind legs he would have stood ten, maybe eleven feet high. That's one big bear!" Ben took the Winchester off the shelf, unwrapped it and showed it to Carruthers. The Mountie worked the action and handed it back to Ben. "It's still in good shape. It's yours."

As the others looked around the cave, Ben stepped outside, unconsciously listening for alarm calls. Then, for the last time, he climbed the trail to the lookout, hoping to see Wolf. But nothing moved in the valley that he could see. He would have liked to have stayed and searched for Wolf, but they were in the valley only for the day.

Ben took his mother and the Mountie further down the valley. When they passed the cottonwood tree, he made no comment about his night of terror, even though he could still see the deep gouges dug into the trunk by the grizzly's massive claws. It was a personal thing.

Arriving at the cabin site, Ben showed the Mountie where John was buried, and he took pictures for his report. Ben took out a bronze plaque from his packsack and placed it on the grave:

JOHN SAUNDERS

HUSBAND OF LAURA

Ben reached in his pocket and pulled out John's pocket watch. Opening the cover, he showed his mother the inscription inside, then he placed the watch on the grave marker. Mom squeezed his hand and nodded in agreement.

"It's over, John," Ben said softly. "I wish you and Laura peace."

Shortly after Ben had walked out of the wilderness, the Mountie had identified the prospector as John Saunders. His wife, Laura, died in a boating accident in 1939. John had no known relatives so he was left where Ben buried him.

The Canadian government, along with bush pilots from Yukon and Northwest Territories, British Columbia, and Alaska, searched for Dan, but his plane was never found.

According to Tlingit tradition, the Wolf Clan gave a potlatch to honor Ben's grandfather and invited Ben, his mother, and Constable Carruthers as honored guests. The clan sang the mourning song. As part of the ceremony, they presented Ben with a dance blanket and gave him his Indian name: *Gooch Du Keek*, Wolf Brother. Moved by the outpouring of love for his grandfather by the clan, Ben finally felt at peace. But the valley of the grizzly would always be a part of him.

# AUTHOR'S NOTES

I set Ben's story in the lost wilderness of northern British Columbia of fifty years ago. In those days, that section of B.C. encompassed a wilderness the size of California. In addition, communications and search and rescue operations lacked the sophistication of their modern counterparts. These elements added up to a likely setting for a survival story.

Many of the events in the novel mirror real-life incidents. The skeleton Ben found was based on the discovery of the mummified body of a trapper who was attacked by a grizzly. Crawling back to his cabin and into his bunk, the trapper scrawled a note: "Have ben tore up by a bear no show to get out. Good by." Unable to stand the pain, he shot himself with a .45 Colt revolver.

Ben's character was loosely based on a true story from an early-day newspaper about a boy who had been abandoned during the gold rush, but was befriended by a band of Indians. I also patterned Ben's adventures on a Tlingit Indian boy who fought an Alaskan brown bear with a knife.

Ben's scalp wound was typical of a grizzly attack. In my files are several accounts of scalps either being torn loose or bitten off. A young friend of mine was blinded in a bear attack.

Cyrus Paul's character was a composite of several traditional Tlingit men I have known over the years. They spoke fluent Tlingit, and reflected the old values of the land and the Tlingit's spiritual relationship to that land. Cyrus Paul's encounter with a grizzly "who bit me to teach me a lesson," reflects traditional Tlingit belief that if you talk about harming a bear, he will come for you. Hooting of an owl was considered bad luck, and in Cyrus's case was equivalent to: "I heard the owl call my name." This is the belief in some northwest tribes that an owl calls the name of a person when it is his\her time to die.

Wolf's character was based on a dominant two-year-old male who had left the pack, looking for a mate to form his own pack. This type of animal does not accept an inferior position in wolf hierarchy. Less aggressive animals stay with the group in a rigid order of dominance. Wolf was a gray wolf, the only species that barks.

The mournful howl Wolf made from the top of the knoll overlooking the Mountie station was an, "I am alone" call. This howl can be heard when a wolf is separated from the pack. When a wolf finds a dead wolf, he will howl a "death howl." This is the howl Wolf made after he and Ben saw the valley after the storm. I took some poetic license in setting that scene.

The grizzly is the most dangerous animal in North America. I have run across them many times in the Alaskan and Canadian back country. In most cases they get out of my way, but not all the time. For example, my partner and I were hiking in the British Columbia gold rush country in the early 1960s, and we jumped a grizzly with two cubs. Immediately, she broke in a lunging charge, swerving off the trail just as I was getting ready to shoot. Stopping about fifty feet from us, the grizzly paced us, huffing and popping her teeth until we turned a bend in the trail. Contrary to popular belief, the grizzly does not normally growl.

Duane Peterson, an Alaskan guide, said that in all his years as a guide, he heard only one bear make a growling noise. John Joyce, a biologist for the Alaska Department for Fish and Game, was charged by a brown bear, and the animal "roared like a lion." John had to shoot the brownie and it fell at his feet.

Prospectors and trappers in Yukon Territory and Alaska have had many encounters with grizzlies. In my collection, I have one hundred accounts of grizzly maulings, many of them ending in death. In 1920, Thomas W. Hammon, a U.S. Commissioner at Iliamna, Alaska, wrote a letter to the Governor of the Territory of Alaska stating: ". . . I have known of more than a hundred white men and natives being killed or crippled by brown bears. . . ."

Ed Ferrell

Juneau, Alaska

CPSIA information can be obtained at www.ICGtesting.com
Printed in the USA
BVOW080507041011

272612BV00007B/1/P